RICHARD RENE

The Ordeal of Windfire

Tales from Mysterion, Book 3

Contents

Join My Reader's Group! v

Prologue vi

I Part One

Chapter One 3
Disagree 6
Chapter Two 12
Disagree 28
Chapter Three 34
Disagree 44
Chapter Four 52
Disagree 69
Chapter Five 79
Disagree 94

II Part Two

Chapter Six 109
Chapter Seven 119
Chapter Eight 126
Chapter Nine 133
Chapter Ten 138
Chapter Eleven 144

Chapter Twelve 151

Chapter Thirteen 157

Chapter Fourteen 165

III Part Three

Chapter Fifteen 173

Chapter Sixteen 176

Chapter Seventeen 187

Chapter Eighteen 191

Chapter Nineteen 201

Chapter Twenty 205

Chapter Twenty-One 216

Did you enjoy this book? You can make a big difference! 223

Join My Reader's Group!

Building a relationship with my readers is one of the best parts of the writing life. I send out occasional newsletters to my Readers' Group with interesting curated content, as well as details of new releases in the Tales of Mysterion and special offers.

You can find the link to sign up for my Readers' Group at the end of this novel.

Prologue

The girl arrived late at the cemetery. She stepped out from the predawn shadows, and the waning moon ignited her tangled mop of blonde hair like a beacon. Instead of running, as she had so many times before, she took even, measured steps. Her feet easily traced the familiar path among the grave markers to the one she knew so well, which lay at the edge of the cemetery, backing up against the forest.

Isabella Morgan gazed at the surface of the headstone, its inscription so faded that it no longer really fulfilled its function. She bent and traced the inscription with her finger as her lips formed the words:

Jean De Sagré

She had known this man in another life, the life she had left weeks before. Her memories of Mysterion—she struggled now to recall its name—had slipped through the fingers of her mind like silt under a torrent of water. Everything about the man, except his name, had also faded. And yet somehow his immense presence had continued to float in the darkness just behind her consciousness—the reservoir of strength on which she had drawn to go back home and at last confront her mother's tears and the rage of her father, who said he would kill her the next time she ever pulled a knife on him.

She had met his eyes without flinching. "I will never touch you again. And you will never touch *me* again."

"Baby," her mother began, "your father didn't mean . . ."

"Enough, *maman*," Isabella said. "It's time to face things as they are."

"You talk to us like that?" her father said. "Damn you, we're your parents!"

"Maybe one day. But not today. Today, you have choice."

Her father took a step toward her. "You little . . ."

"You have a choice," she repeated. "You can call Auntie Marie and ask her to take me for a while, maybe a year or two, or else I go to the police right now and report both of you for neglect and abuse."

Her father gaped. Her mother put her hands to her face and started sobbing.

"What kind of child are you?" her father said. "Report your own parents to the police?"

The trembling had come over Isabella then, and she had wavered. Then an image had surfaced, a memory from Mysterion: her hand gripping a hatchet, holding it high in the air; Disagree's huge black hand enfolding hers, and both of them bringing the hatchet down to cut the rope that held her in Mysterion . . .

She met her father's eyes. "I have lost everything. I'll do anything to get it back."

Her father had hesitated then, his eyes shifting, and she knew she had won. They had called Auntie Marie that same afternoon. In the weeks it had taken to finalize the arrangements, Isabella had taken Jonah's advice and stayed at home. But although she left the house before dawn and returned long after dark, gobbling down her cold leftover supper with her eyes lowered before hurrying to her bedroom, she had not been able to avoid her father's sullenness and the accusation in her mother's eyes.

The meetings with Jonah had been her only island of relief.

A rustling behind her interrupted the chirrup of the crickets. She straightened without haste just as Jonah stumbled out of the undergrowth. Isabella smiled, the moonlight throwing her pale, hungry features into sharp relief. He had missed the path again. He did not know the way here as well as she did. In the past weeks, he had preferred to meet at the beach, where he kept the Lamp. Something about the sound of the waves, he said, that regular breathing of water would help her learn to kindle it.

Tonight, she had called him, and he was lost. She smiled. She would surprise him. Tonight, they would do it her way.

Jonah made his way among the neglected gravestones, reaching out to steady himself when he tripped. As he reached her side, Isabella noted beads of sweat on his forehead. The air was close and damp, like a fist.

"I don't understand," Jonah panted, "why we have to do this so early. You're lucky I got to the phone before my mother did!"

"I told you," Isabella said. "I have to try one more time before Auntie comes to get me."

"You know I can always come visit," Jonah said. "La Digue is not that far."

"Do you think that once Auntie gets her hands on me, she's going to let me have anything to do with anyone from this life? You can bet it'll be nothing but wake up, do whatever slave tasks she has for me, go to school, come back, do my homework, go to bed, and go to Mass on Sundays. I wouldn't be surprised if she asks the priest to baptize me again, just to make sure. It has to happen now."

"Or else what?"

"Or else I'm done."

Jonah smiled. "I don't believe that, not from you. You want to get back. That's why you came here," he gestured around. "You needed him. You needed him to be close to you. To help you kindle the Lamp."

"Yes," she said, staring at the gravestone. "He died long ago, but I know he can help me now. I don't understand that."

Jonah paused before answering. "No one is dead," he said. "Not really. Everyone is still alive in another time."

She met his eyes. Jonah had understood her heart—again. Something passed between them, and she felt her cheeks beginning to flush. Jonah too must have felt something. He broke eye contact and busied himself unslinging a knapsack, opening the drawstring and pulling out the Lamp, ornate and shining in the moonlight. He placed it on the grave, where it stood like a miniature domed temple.

"Why don't we get you back to find him then?" he said.

Isabella smiled, and this time her face softened. "Thank you."

His shrug was slightly exaggerated. "Oh, don't thank me. This is exactly what your parents have been paying me for, don't you know—to follow their crazy daughter into cemeteries at midnight . . ."

"That's not funny."

"Sorry," he said. He squatted down. Isabella sat opposite, cross-legged, with her back to Jean De Sagré's gravestone.

The Lamp sat between them.

The leaves rustled as an overhead breeze passed through. The sluggish air shifted and moved around them briefly.

"Ready?" Jonah said.

Isabella nodded.

Jonah lifted the Lamp until the middle—a lattice-work

screen that encircled and connected the top with the base—was level with Isabella's face. She closed her eyes briefly, then looked directly through the gaps in the lattice into the darkness at the center of the Lamp. She leaned against Jean De Sagré's stone. The cool immovable surface held her up as he had somehow done in another life.

Jonah shifted to keep the lattice grill close to her face. Isabella could see that he wanted to say something, to advise her on her posture—*when you kindle the Lamp you need to sit straight*—but he restrained himself and she was grateful to him for not correcting her. Since he had first shown her the Lamp, many months ago now, she had surprised herself at her eagerness to absorb everything he had to teach. And still, she had not managed to kindle the flame whose source inside the Lamp she had never been able to discover.

Tonight, it will be different, she thought. *Because of* him. *We never came here because I forgot that he was here to help.*

"Help me, Dis," she said, not knowing why she called him that. And she exhaled into the Lamp.

A flame flickered to life inside the space enclosed by the lattice work. It seemed to hover in the darkness, its light held back, hesitating. She continued to blow. The flame strengthened, radiated to touch her face, intensifying the hunger in her features as she stared into the center of the Lamp. Anyone watching might expect her to run out of breath, but Isabella blew long after it was humanly possible, as if somehow her lungs had expanded beyond the dimensions of her skinny frame.

Jonah watched her. In the intensifying light of the Lamp, he was smiling.

The space around them, encompassing Jean De Sagré's grave,

x

was a sphere of daylight. Every detail—the s-shaped crack in the stone, the grass flattened in the spot where Isabella had sat so many times—thrown into sharp relief, seemed more real somehow than they ever had in daylight.

Isabella continued to blow.

The sphere expanded, slowed, hesitated, then exploded suddenly outward in a rushing wave. For an instant, the tiny, forgotten cemetery was caught in brilliance more penetrating than the noonday sun. The explosion caught Isabella, bearing her upwards. She looked down, saw herself still staring into the Lamp, Jonah holding it before her, both of them cocooned in an egg of Lamplight nesting in the forest.

Then the vision shrank away as she rose, spiraling away, borne on the light that swirled and eddied over her skin like water.

I

Part One

Chapter One

The stream of Okean flows over Mysterion as over a rounded pebble. Driven by the dark winds of Chaos, its golden surface roils with silent turbulence as it rises from the west and descends into the east, before flowing down beneath the world to the place of the Lethes, where it begins its cycle of return all over again.

While darkness rules Chaos above Okean, the stream itself—known to some as "water-above-the-heavens"—radiates its own light, cloaking itself in a thin mantle of eternal day to resist the darkness pressing down from above. In this realm, the Angeli keep watch over the world, bearing witness to life and death. The wing-covered Elementals patrol the surface as they look down into Okean's crystal depths—down through the dome that holds the stars, the moon, and the sun—and further down still to the immense, polished shield of Mysterion, its features chiseled by some heavenly metalsmith.

As Isabella kindled the Lamp deep beneath the world, in the place of the Lethes, a pair of Angeli hovered over the eastern Edge of Okean, at the place where it began its downward flow toward the Falls. Though huddled close together as if engaged in a private conversation, the Angeli were silent, their attention fixed on a spot on the ocean of Mysterion. To ordinary eyes there was nothing there but water, faintly speckled. But Angeli have the ability to magnify the sight of distant objects, so they could make out with perfect clarity a small oblong island, and a rowing skiff pulled up on its shore.

"Why did you leave them there?" one said at last.

"I was just doing what I was told," the other replied. "I got them clear. They can find their own way from there."

"There are other islands," the first Angelus said with a sly tone. "Why this one?"

"Are you suggesting that I am interfering, Shantiel?"

"I know you, Azrel," Shantiel said. Something like a smile touched over the Angelus's features. "You are always the first to volunteer yourself when the Wind calls for our involvement. More than once you have pushed the limits of your role, and some have even argued for your censure—"

"Ah!" Azrel dismissed the words with a flutter. "They love their laws so much they would censure the Wind Itself!"

Shantiel's smile persisted. "So, you had no ulterior motive in bringing the Elder and Sartish to Qatala's island?"

Azrel looked sideways at Shantiel. "Well . . ."

"I knew it," Shantiel said.

"I was hoping that they might find some counsel," Azrel said. "Some way to take back the island. That's all."

"And then?" Shantiel said.

"I don't know. But the Wind may call us to involve ourselves. Will you help?" she said, with a touch of pleading.

"I don't know," Shantiel sighed. "I'm already blacklisted just being your friend. Most of them don't talk to me."

"They're boring anyway," Azrel said. "You have much more fun with me."

Shantiel laughed. "That's true, I suppose. But still, Azrel—be careful. The Wind has given us a role, keep watch and bear witness. The ways things are going, you risk being shunned as a lawbreaker."

"If it comes to a choice between a law and the life of a friend," Azrel said, "I would choose the friend any day."

Shantiel shook her head. "That's exactly the problem. You're an Angelus, but you're talking like a human."

"They were made to rule the Elementals, weren't they?" Azrel said. "Nothing wrong with emulating your leaders."

Shantiel's wings made a gesture reminiscent of thrown up hands. "You always have an argument ready, don't you?"

"Of course," Azrel replied, grinning. "Now, back to it. I don't want to miss something."

And the Angeli fell silent, turning their attention back to the surface of the world below.

Disagree

Where the stream of Okean meets the eastern Edge of Mysterion, the dome of the sky runs like wet paint down to join the horizon. Mingling with water, it falls to the base of the world and into the place where the Lethes sleep. Along the Falls, a cloud of mist billows up, enveloped in a deafening thunder. It was through this cloud that a skiff inched late one night, working against the dark water that rushed toward the Falls.

Most rowers could not resist the grip of the current. Once it got hold of you, it would not let go. And even this rower, remarkable as he was, had to pull hard without pausing, the sweat trickling down his bald head into his eyes, to make even the slightest progress back toward safety beyond the reef.

The truth was that, under normal circumstances, Disagree could not have summoned the strength to haul on the oars with such persistence. But tonight, he poured everything he had into the work, pitting the dark tide of his grief against the water that threatened to drive the skiff backwards at any moment.

Ever since he had come from the Tree, this had been his way. He had concealed the movements of his heart from the others, channeling them into whatever task the king had given him in that moment. That was how everyone came to know him as the king's rock—an inscrutable stone who felt nothing and acted with a decisiveness that no one would dare resist. But the king knew, and eventually, Bella did too.

Disagree had known from the beginning that it was a mistake to open his heart to her, but the loneliness of her wandering the camp at nights like a stray cat had reminded him of his own first days among the Brethren. She noticed him too, because one day he found her beside him when he was on sentry duty. He said nothing, nor did she, but it didn't matter. Before he had been entirely aware of it, they were friends.

Friendship was dangerous. She had known how to hurt him, and being the wounded creature that she was, she did it often. Small betrayals, cutting remarks, denigrations—she did it all, sometimes out of anger, at other times out of a sheer spiteful joy, because she could. But behind it all he knew was the test.

Would he remain her friend even if she did *this*, or said *that*?

He had remained, unmoved and unmoving, and she had come back with a beseeching somewhere in her blue eyes that she could not bring herself to speak out loud. How many times had she come and gone, angry and lashing out, only to slip back to his side in the dawn, high from smoking powdered dragon's claw?

He heaved a deep breath as he thought about it. He had known better than to say anything about that filthy habit.

"I had a father," she would say, *"and after that hell I don't need another one."*

Then the king had sent her to kill the tyrant. He had arranged everything so that she would throw herself into it, and nothing Disagree had said could dissuade her. The king had wanted to test her, see if she could prove herself worthy of his throne. When Disagree protested, Hodoul's eyes had hardened and he had drawn back behind that cold and ruined countenance that he showed to everyone else.

"You are presuming on my generosity, Monsieur Disagree," he had said.

"But you say before you do not want to put the girl in danger—"

"Never mistake a soft heart for a soft head. And never make the mistake of thinking that I possess either, understand?"

Disagree understood. In offhand moments, when wine cracked that rigid carapace of his, the king had let slip how much he cared for Bella, a feeling he concealed from everyone, even himself most of the time. Still, he never wanted to be reminded that anyone knew, and Disagree had learned to play along.

When the king sent Bella to kill the tyrant, it had been his test for her. When she had failed to meet his expectations, only Disagree understood how much his rage had been fueled by disappointment and a broken heart.

To compound the wound, Disagree had helped her escape . . . Even now Disagree could evoke with clarity her thin hand, holding up the hatchet over the cable that tethered the tyrant's ship to Mysterion. Her pale hungry face, so different than his own, had looked up at him as she whispered, *Take it all away from me.*

And he had done it. He had enfolded her thin bony fist with his and brought the hatchet down with all his weight. Moments later, he was rowing away from the ship with the king, who was furious at him for helping the girl, but too fearful to refuse his help in escaping the Falls. Disagree had last seen the schooner plunging broadside toward the Falls as Isabella grappled the spinning wheel, trying to control it . . .

Disagree blinked and shook his head, trying to rid his mind of the memory, and for the first time he stopped rowing.

The dark figure of Hodoul, hunched in the stern, stirred and raised his bushy head. "Don't stop, damn you. Pull!"

Disagree regarded Hodoul. He couldn't make out his face through the darkness and mist, but he could imagine the baleful expression in the king's stone-grey eyes. "Why? You order me dead as soon as we get back."

"Perhaps you are hoping for mercy," Hodoul said. "By the Code I can give you none. You knew how important she was to me and you let her escape. You betrayed me, and the punishment for betrayal is death by hanging!"

"Perhaps we go back to the Falls then," Disagree said. He jerked his head at the thick bank of mist behind them and the thunder of the Falls, still loud enough that they had to raise their voices to make themselves heard.

Despite himself, Hodoul glanced over the side. The skiff's forward momentum had died as soon as Disagree had stopped rowing. Now they drifted backwards, losing the gains of the past hour in seconds. "You will not let that happen," he said. "You have no desire to return to the chains of slavery in the lower world, just as I have no desire to return to the drumroll and the jeering crowd and the hangman's noose. You will keep rowing to save your skin!" There was a touch of desperation in his voice now.

"If I row," Disagree said, ignoring the skiff as it spun broadside before the current. "That is not the reason. I come from the lower world to be free. If I row, it is for you. You never understand this, and perhaps you never do. But still I do it . . ." He shook his head.

"Of course you do it for me," Hodoul said. "You owe me. If it wasn't for me, you'd have been dead twenty years by now!"

"No," Disagree said. "That debt is paid many times over.

That is not the reason."

The roaring had intensified. The skiff bucked, racing head-long toward the Falls. At any moment, the cloud would break, just before the meeting of Okean and the sea. No amount of rowing would save them then.

"Damn you!" Hodoul shouted. His hands gripped the boat as if trying to turn it by sheer force of will. "Will you do as I say?"

"Yes, of course," Disagree said. "But first, tell me. You really do not understand why?"

"I don't know!" Hodoul screamed. "Pity? Is that it?"

Disagree sighed. He lowered the oars, and dug into the current, forcing the bow around. The skiff resisted him, like a wild horse feeling the lasso, and then complied. With Disagree working again, their backward rush slowed, and stopped. Minutes later, they were inching their way back toward the reef.

"So, it *was* pity," Hodoul said. The darkness hid the sneer on his lips. "I should have known. Pity has always been your weakness, and one day it will be your death. Perhaps that day should have been today, if I were in my right mind. Still . . ." he paused. "I suppose I can be magnanimous. No one else witnessed your treason but me and the girl. And you are no doubt aware that I would give no second chance . . ."

Disagree did not reply. His stroke was strong and even, and they were making more progress even than before.

"So, I offer you clemency," Hodoul said, spreading his arms. "You will live. For now, at least. But the slightest disobedience, and you will dance at the end of a rope, just like when you were a boy. Do you understand?"

Disagree was silent.

"Do you understand?" Hodoul snapped.

"Yes," Disagree said.

"Good. Now, put your back into it. I want to weigh anchor by dawn. This excursion has taken us away too long. By the time we get back, who knows what mischief those princes will have gotten up to. I will need to set the house in order, and I will require your assistance to do so. That will be your first test."

"I obey you," Disagree said. "Even to my own death. But not because I pity you. *You* do not understand that."

Hodoul laughed. "Frankly, Disagree, I do not care to know your reasons for obeying. Just so long as you obey."

Chapter Two

Jonah watched Isabella blow into the Lamp. Her face had lost its usual hunger and acquired a serenity he had never seen before. For the first time, she was truly beautiful, a fact that threatened to distract him from his focus.

The light from the Lamp's wick had pushed back the darkness, forming a cocoon within which everything was not merely lit up, thrown into sharp relief, but also enhanced, more real and vibrant than before.

Now she has it, Jonah thought. Why didn't I think of coming to this place with her?

Before he could reflect on it, the Lamplight exploded in a blinding brilliance, and . . .

* * *

Jonah opened his eyes. The deep aquamarine of the morning sky filled his vision. A few horsetails streamed far above. The morning sun, well risen, beat down on his face, already raising sweat on his forehead.

Jonah sat up, still groggy from sleep. It still took him time to bring his awareness back to Mysterion when he woke from the world of the Lethes. He had to remind himself that he had in fact woken from a dream.

Then he realized—*She did it!*

He had descended to the Lethes every night for the past three years, since the Elder had named him New Elder. However long he lived with them, in times throughout their history and places all over their world, his work never lasted more than one night's sleep in Mysterion. Sometimes he woke with a heaviness, knowing that the Lethes would stay buried beneath the world for now, lost in dreaming. At other times, Jonah sat up with joy coursing through him and ran to pull them from the Seeing Pools.

Today was one of those days, but more intense. Isabella had been special. She had taken more from him—and given more back. Jonah would not go so far as to say he had wanted her to learn the Lamp more than the others he had instructed. Still, her achievement was somehow sweeter, as if he had learned it all over again.

Now Isabella would be unburied, but he would not be there to witness it. Perhaps Shantih, faithful as always, would be the one to take her from the Pool. And then there was old Pierre, doing his best to hold everything together until Jonah returned . . . The anxiousness to return to the island tugged Jonah back to the present.

Time to get going, he thought. He wondered if he should wake Sartish. His companion was curled up in a fetal position amidships, frowning in his sleep. Last night, he had been hauling on the oars while Azrel towed their skiff on a line away from the Falls, her brilliant fluttering form pushing back the mist and darkness as she flew forward. She and Sartish were embarked on one of their arguments: whether or not the human need for sleep was a weakness. Azrel claimed that it most certainly was, given that it hampered—for instance—a human's ability to row his own feeble self to safety without turning one of the noblest creatures in Mysterion into a mere beast of burden. As Jonah fell into sleep, Sartish was saying something to the effect that he could row all night just fine without her help . . .

Jonah smiled. Sartish must have conceded the argument in the end.

And speaking of that, Jonah thought. *Where is the loud-mouthed one?*

He looked around. Azrel had disappeared, which wasn't unusual. She would return when needed, as she always did. More interesting to him was the place the Angelus had chosen to leave them. After they left the ship, Jonah had instructed her to take them to nearest safe harbor. Now their skiff rested high on a narrow beach that encircled a dome-like island. The sides of the island rose steeply above them, all scrub and tangled coconut grass and vines. Jonah could just make out a small, dense copse at the very top. Other than the hiss of waves onto the sand, and the far-away cries of birds, all was quiet.

Sartish cried out, jerked in his sleep, and sat up. Jonah saw that his shirt was drenched with sweat, clinging to his skin. Sartish stared at Jonah, not seeing him, then looked around. He shook his head, trying to clear it.

"The dream again?" Jonah asked.

Sartish nodded once, abruptly. Jonah didn't need to ask. Since leaving the Brethren, Sartish had been haunted by a dream of his life among the Lethes. He had told Jonah about Uncle Sat, who burned his arms with a cigarette when he disobeyed—and sometimes even when he didn't, just to prove a point.

Jonah knew better than to say anything when Sartish woke from that dream. Until the memory of it receded, he turned back into the kind of boy he must have been among the Brethren—truculent and easily provoked.

"Where are we?" Sartish muttered, his word slurring.

"One of the Solitary Islands," Jonah said.

Sartish looked around. "So, the Angelus just left us here and disappeared?"

Jonah shrugged. "Angeli come and go as they please. She'll be back."

Sartish frowned. "But why wasn't she taking us all the way back home?"

"If I were to guess," Jonah said, "I would say Azrel thought we might need some advice on how to proceed."

"What advice?" Sartish said. "We return to the island and use the Lamp to blast those filthy pirates into dust!"

Jonah shook his head. "That's just it. We cannot use the Lamp in that way."

"The Elder was using—"

"The Elder used the Lamp against the Djinn. These are not Djinn. If they come against the Lamp, that's one thing—" Jonah paused, a cloud of sadness touching his face as he relived the memory—"But I won't use it as a weapon against human beings, even despicable, degenerate ones like the Brethren."

"So, what then?" Sartish asked. "Go and sit on the mountaintop for the rest of our lives, waiting for them to leave?"

"Forget that!" Jonah said. "We must break the siege. But we need help, and that's why Azrel brought us here. I think."

"It seems circuitous to me," Sartish said.

"Sometimes the Wind blows in circles," Jonah replied. "All we can do is follow." To forestall further argument—which he knew would go nowhere—Jonah leaped out of the skiff and onto the sand.

"This is a waste of time," Sartish complained.

"At the very least, we can restock our food," Jonah said. "Come on. The sooner we do this, the sooner we can get back."

He strode away. Sartish hesitated before clambering out of the boat after him.

They followed the curve of the island, Jonah searching the slopes for a path as Sartish brooded in his footsteps. Despite his best efforts to shake the memory, the nightmare replayed itself. Uncle Sat held his arm down on the kitchen table—it was made of Formica, pink roses on a white background—and pushed the lit end of his cigarette into his skin, burning all the way through to the tabletop. Seeing the burn mark in the Formica, Uncle Sat had screamed, *You little scoundrel, you are ruining my beautiful table*, and Sartish had cried, because he was sorry about burning the table. He hadn't meant to do it . . .

Then he realized that he and Uncle Sat were at the bottom of a dark hole, with an opening of light far above. He wanted to reach that light, and rose toward it. But his uncle's voice went on screaming in his ear. Even as he ascended toward the opening, the screaming held him like a rubber band, stretching until it brought him to a standstill, just at the edge of the opening, before drawing him back into the hole.

And again, he was sitting at the kitchen table as his uncle pressed that burning tip into the surface of his skin . . .

Geist had come to visit after a particularly painful encounter with Uncle Sat. The Elder Djinn had offered escape and a chance for revenge, and Sartish had taken the dark pendant. He had paid a high price in the Tree—months of torment living out the same nightmare over and over, as it drained his memories of his former life. Then the pirate king had come for him, before the last of his memories could be taken from him. Among the

Brethren, his sleep from then on was a dark void that consumed him at night and relinquished him in the morning.

When he escaped the Brethren and found his way to Elder's Island, Jonah had journeyed with him to the Falls. In time, he was unburied as one of the People. Since then, the nightmare had sometimes come to him, but rarely enough that he could put the horror of it behind him when he woke. Then Isabella had come to assassinate Jonah, and in a fit of madness, Jonah had invited her to do it—if she dared. Something about that had disturbed Sartish. For the first time, he thought about his betrayal of king Hodoul and the Brethren. He had started to wonder if he would always be a traitor . . . The nightmare returned nightly, Sartish finding it more and more difficult to shake it off when he woke.

What was it about that girl? A vision floated before his eyes: her tangled mop of hair in the lamplight as they rowed away from the ship, just before it went over the Falls . . . Was it just last night? Sartish wondered what had happened to her. Secretly, he hoped that she would never be unburied from the place of the Lethes.

"So . . ." he said out loud. "Were you accomplishing your task . . . in the sleep?"

Jonah smiled over his shoulder. "Is that a roundabout way of asking if Isabella learned how to kindle the Lamp?"

Sartish shrugged.

"Yes," Jonah said. "She will be unburied."

"I see," Sartish said.

"Let go of your distrust, Sartish," Jonah said. "She is one of the People now."

Sartish sniffed. "I know the damned pirates, and they are always turning one way or another. Not to be trusted."

Jonah inclined his head. "Yes, she will probably struggle with that for the rest of her life. And so will you, my friend."

"Why are you trusting me, then?" Sartish demanded. "If you do not know which way I will turn today or tomorrow?"

Jonah smiled in that maddening way of his. "It wouldn't be trust if I knew for certain, would it? Look, some vines!"

Thick ropes of plaited vegetation dangled down the side of the island from the top.

"Whoever lives here must have made them," Jonah said. He grabbed one of the ropes and hauled himself upwards, hooking his feet into the vegetation to gain purchase. Sartish watched him, then shook his head. Grabbing another rope, he jerked on it to make sure it would take his weight and started up after Jonah.

They climbed in silence, the sun beating on them. Stewing on the news that Isabella was unburied, Sartish fell behind. When a fly buzzed past his head, he was lost in the turmoil of his thoughts and paid it no attention. It passed again, closer this time. Drawn out of himself, Sartish swiped at the insect. It flew away, but it returned almost immediately to hover beside his ear. A voice—rasping and deep—spoke with unnatural loudness, sounding almost inside his head. "Do you really trust him?"

Sartish cried out, swatting around his head and almost losing his grip on the rope.

"What's wrong?" Jonah called from above, looking down.

Sartish looked around, frowning as his heart pounded. The fly was gone, leaving only the sound of wind and water.

"Sartish!" Jonah said.

Sartish looked up, his expression bewildered. "Noth—nothing. Keep going!"

Jonah went on, and after looking around one more time, Sartish took up the climb once more. A few minutes later, the slope started to level enough for him to stand upright and relinquish the handholds. Then he stood at the top and came up beside Jonah, panting, the sweat pouring in rivulets down his forehead.

"Are you alright?" Jonah asked. He sounded worried.

"Fine," Sartish muttered. "Fine. Keep moving."

Jonah waited, as if making sure, then led the way into a dense copse of banana and breadfruit trees that resounded with birdsong and rustled with the movements of creatures in the undergrowth. They followed an almost invisible foot trail into the vegetation. The bushes tugged at them with thorns until the vegetation gave way to a small clearing with a lean-to shack woven from coconut fronds at its center.

A short, shriveled old woman wearing nothing but a tattered shift ducked out of the low doorway as they stepped into the clearing. Her skin, burned black by the sun, contrasted with a shock of frizzy white hair that bounced in a joyful profusion from her head. She carried a tray with a jug, cups, and a plate of fresh fruit and nuts.

"Azrel said you would come soon!" she cried. "Come and sit!"

The sight of the food and drink overcame any hesitations they might have had. They sat and tucked in gratefully. When the plate was empty, the old woman hurried inside to refill it. At last, they sat back, sated. The dark mood from the previous night receded from Sartish's mind. He wondered if the voice he had heard had been just some kind of hallucination, inspired by lack of food and water.

"Good?" the old woman said.

Jonah nodded. "Thank you for receiving us, Wise Mother."

The old woman raised one hand. "I am just an old woman learning how to be a human being. Mine is yours."

"Then we must ask for one more thing of yours," Jonah said.

"What is that?"

"Your guidance."

The old woman sucked her lips and looked around vaguely. "Azrel was telling me some things, but I didn't understand . . . The truth is, I understand very little, you see. I don't even remember my true name. Qatala calls me 'Tala,' but that was not my name before. How can I help with your affairs?"

Jonah explained. After he finished, Tala was silent.

"They are safe, are they not?" she said at last. "They are protected by the Lamp?"

Jonah hesitated. "Yes . . . But they are besieged, trapped."

Tala shook her head. "I do not understand much, but I do know that everything can be conquered by stillness."

Sartish looked at Jonah. *I told him this was a waste of our time!*

Jonah kept his eyes fixed on Tala. "Isn't there another way?"

Tala's bright black eyes moved from him to Sartish, considering something.

"Perhaps Qatala may have a word for you," she said finally. She rose to her feet. "Come. We will have to wake her."

Moving at a crablike speed a that belied her age, bent over and without looking back, Tala hastened her way into the forest. Jonah and Sartish scrambled up and ran to keep her in sight. Shoving their way through the undergrowth, they soon lost sight of her, following the sound of loud rustling from ahead.

"This is pointless," Sartish grumbled, dragging himself through yet another fern bush that tugged at him with its thorns. "They are Solitaries. What else are they going to tell us but stay where we are and be quiet?"

"Azrel had a reason for bringing us here," Jonah said stubbornly.

Maybe she was just giving up on us," Sartish said. But before he could elaborate on the thought, they emerged from the forest. The island had ended, the grass and moss dropping sheer to the water below. At the edge of the cliff, Tala waited motionless, but as they started toward her, she raised a warning hand.

"Stand back a little," she said. "She sometimes snaps at strangers."

Leaning out over the cliff, she called, "Qatala!"

There was no response. Sartish threw another dark look at Jonah.

"Now she's talking into thin air," he murmured. "Are you seeing this?"

"Qatala!" Tala called again.

Jonah took a step forward and started to say something to Tala. As he did, the ground shifted beneath their feet. Sartish and Jonah teetered, almost tumbled over, waving their arms to keep their balance. By contrast, Tala moved easily in harmony with earthquake, as if she had experienced it all before.

Nearby, a banana tree went over with a crash. At the edge of the cliff, a chunk of grass, earth, and moss slipped off and fell away into the sea below, exposing a hard surface, covered in regular, familiar patterns.

All at once, Sartish recognized what he was looking at. "It's a shell!"

The earth beneath them shifted again, and this time they did fall, clutching the ground in terror. A turtle's head the size of a house rose into view, craning around to regard them with inscrutable eyes like pools of tar.

"What is it, my dear?" the turtle said. "You know I was sleeping!" She kept her eyes fixed on the two boys, but she was obviously speaking to Tala. Under that gaze, neither Sartish nor Jonah dared move.

"The Angelus brought them, my dear," Tala said.

"More visitors?" the turtle cried. "With all these people running around, we will soon no longer be solitary!"

"They want a word from you, my dear."

"What word?"

"You remember what the Angelus was saying better than I do, my dear."

Qatala frowned, the wrinkles on her already impossibly wrinkled head deepening as she tried to recall the conversation.

Then, comprehension dawned. "Oh! But why? Did they not like your word?"

Tala glanced at Jonah and Sartish. "I think . . . they wanted another word, my dear."

"Did they, now?" Qatala said. "Well, there is only one other word. If they cannot stay still, they must fight, mustn't they?"

"That is what I was saying," Sartish said.

"No," Jonah said firmly. "Our Lethes ancestors joined forces with the Djinn and fought their own brothers and sisters. Now that they are unburied, the People of the Wind will never fight in war again."

"If they will not stay still, and they will not fight," Qatala growled, "then they must find someone to fight for them."

"What about a way of peace?" Jonah asked.

Sartish cringed inside. *Now he is begging . . .*

"No," Qatala said. "There is no other word!" Tala shook her head in agreement.

Jonah stared at her. Then his shoulders sagged.

"What did I say?" Sartish said. "You see? We might as well fight for ourselves!"

Jonah took a deep breath. "The Elder gave me a responsibility. I cannot use his Lamp to destroy human beings . . ." As Sartish opened his mouth to object, he continued, "But I won't throw my island and my People to the pirates either." He squared his shoulders. "Can you help us find someone to fight on our behalf?"

Qatala's eyelids drooped, half concealing her eyes. She looked at Tala, who raised her hands in acquiescence.

"Find the Wandering Sailor," Qatala said. "He will help you."

"The Wandering Sailor," Jonah said, frowning. "You mean, the Elder's companion?"

"The same."

"But he died a long time ago," Jonah said. "Before my time—"

"Then you must seek and wake him in the Cavern of the Sleepers," Qatala said.

Jonah shook his head. "The mermaids won't allow that. Only the dead can go there."

"Then you must join the dead," Qatala said. "I can help you. But you won't enjoy it!" She cackled at her own joke.

Jonah frowned. "How . . .?"

"You want it or not?" Qatala snapped.

"We must decide," Sartish said. "Hodoul is sailing back as we speak. Who knows what he will do to overcome the Lamp?"

Jonah looked agonized. "Yes. We want it."

"What are you doing?" Sartish cried. "You cannot . . ."

"I speak for the People of the Wind," Jonah said, ignoring him. "We want it."

Qatala nodded. "Very well." She turned her eyes on Tala. "Now, my dear, it is time to move. These parts are too busy!"

"Are you sure, my dear?" Tala said, clasping her hands, looking anxious. "You know how much I hate moving . . ."

"I'm afraid so," Qatala replied. She turned away. "Goodbye, small men. May the Wind blow you wherever It will!"

"Time to go, my boys," Tala said, scuttling past them and disappearing into the trees back to her shelter. Qatala's shell quaked and lurched forward, this time throwing them to the ground. The trees whipped around. Right beside them, a large clump of earth and vegetation slid away down the side of the shell.

"She's moving!" Jonah scrambled to his feet. "We have to get back to the boat. Now!"

"You think?" Sartish said.

They raced back where they came, skirting the edge of the forest, dodging the trees that now toppled left and right, their roots easily dislodged in the shallow soil. Cracks opened and chunks of earth slid away as Qatala dislodged herself from the sand on which she had rested for so long. Jonah and Sartish leapt from one to another, but their landing spot shifted as soon as they set foot on it, forcing them to jump again. At last, there was nowhere to go. The last of the trees thrashed and tumbled down toward the water. They stood on the exposed surface of Qatala's shell, a dome of ridged polygonal patterns.

"She's diving!" Jonah said, pointing. Below, the water rose wild and green and foaming up the sides of the shell.

"What do we do?" Sartish shouted in a panic. The waves washed over their feet, rising to their knees. Jonah looked around. There was nothing but ocean in all directions. Qatala must have crushed the skiff as she slid off the sand. They were submerging fast, and once Qatala went under, they would be drawn down with her . . .

"What about Tala?" Sartish said, pointing. Behind them, the old woman's shelter was the only thing left standing. The water lapped at the doorway, but there was no sign of her at all. She intended to go down with Qatala.

"Perhaps she can help!" Jonah said. Together, they waded through the rising water, trying not to slip on the slick surface of the shell. As they approached the doorway, Tala pulled aside the curtain, smiling at them.

"No time for more tea, boys," she said.

"Old Mother, we lost our boat," Jonah panted. "Can you ask Qatala to stop?"

Tala shook her head. "She's helping you. Isn't this what you asked for?"

"Asked for . . .?" he said, bewildered. "No, she was going to help us join—"

Then, with a constriction in his chest, he understood.

"What?" Sartish said, staring at him. "What is it?"

"We have to drown," Jonah said. "It's only way to join the dead."

The water swirled around their waists. The turtle was under. At any moment, the current would draw them under as well.

"You mean . . ." Sartish said. "Commit suicide?"

"No," Jonah said. "Qatala knows the tradition."

Tala laughed and clapped her hands. "You understand!"

"What tradition?" Sartish said. The water had reached his chest.

Jonah gripped the frame of the shelter, holding himself against the swirling current. "The tradition that says the mermaids know when it's your time and when it isn't! Qatala is betting that they'll know it isn't our time!"

"Mermaids . . ." Sartish whispered. Three years earlier, he had helped Jonah escape the Blind Watchman. Bailing from Jonah's boat, he had lightened the hull just enough for it to speed out of the monster's clutches. As he dove for the depths, one of the Blind Watchman's hands had struck him with a glancing blow, knocking him unconscious. He must have drowned, but the mermaids had brought him back and carried him to the sanctuary of Elder's Island. Sartish would never forget the strangeness of coming to life underwater, or the undersea journey that followed. Nor would he want to repeat the experience . . .

"No, not again. I cannot—" he started. The current pushed him off his feet. In desperation, he grabbed at the sinking frame.

"The Wind be with us," Jonah said, his face pale with terror.

"I learned to breathe underwater," Tala said cheerfully. "Maybe you will too!"

Before either of them could respond, the water surged over their heads. As they clung to the shelter—which must have been attached permanently to the shell—Qatala pulled them under, descending with terrifying speed.

Panic took hold of Sartish, and he let go of the frame. Jonah screamed bubbles, grabbed at him, and missed. Sartish spun away into the current and Qatala's wake, but the turtle's vast body continued to suck him into her dive. By the time he came to a stop, the surface was a distant shimmering firmament.

Too far to reach, Sartish thought. His lungs convulsed. He looked down. Qatala was pulling away into the opaque green depths. In the doorway of her shelter, Tala was still visible, looking back and waving. Jonah had relinquished his grip, and now he floated in Qatala's wake, his arms and legs limp.

He's dead, Sartish thought. *And now it's my turn*. His lungs burned. The darkness closed in around him. He watched his last breath rise in a cloud of bubbles toward the surface, a small circle of light above him.

So, this is how I die, he thought. *Just as I did before . . .*

His lungs flooded with water. He struggled, trying to pull for the surface, but not knowing whether he was rising or going deeper. His movements slowed. His limbs twitched. The numbness and heaviness overcame him. The last thing he felt was a single bubble of air brushing past his lips on its way to the surface.

His eyes staring, his limbs spread-eagled, Sartish sank down into the darkness.

Disagree

The Djinn bought the boy named Jean for themselves on the morning that he killed his master, Monsieur Jean-Baptiste De Sagré.

Just after dawn, Jean had descended from the mountain behind the plantation and wound his way through the cinnamon grove, taking the long way back to the slave quarters where he lived with his mothers and sisters.

For the past few weeks, he had escaped the quarters while it was dark to go to his secret place—a platform high on the mountain where a little stream trickled down the rock face. He watched the sun rise in red and gold on the ocean and waited as long as he dared afterward before making his way back down. For his absence, he always received a scolding, but he always timed it close enough to avoid a beating.

Whatever happened, it was a risk he was willing to take. He wanted to be certain he'd been away long enough for Monsieur to leave. The master always arrived at the quarters for his visits after the lamps were extinguished. Everyone knew it was him, of course, but the master, being a man of discretion, went through the motions of anonymity regardless. Since Monsieur had started preferring his mother's room to the others, Jean had left early, to avoid seeing him face-to-face when he left. Somehow, that made things easier to bear. If he didn't see his face, he could almost forget what happened in the night . . .

Women in headscarves and men wearing tattered shorts, their backs already shining with sweat in the early heat, wielded machetes against the cinnamon saplings and hacked the branches into manageable lengths before bundling them for hauling to the drying sheds on the far side of the Big House. Some of them looked up and greeted Jean as he passed, dragging his feet and reaching out to brush the broad green leaves with the tips of his fingers—taking his time. He did not respond to their greetings, but they were used to Silent Jean and accepted the softening of his expression as greeting enough.

He left the cinnamon grove behind and ambled down the slope over the lawn of coconut grass to pass the Big House on his right. It was a large, two-story building with a gently sloping thatched roof and a wide verandah that encircled the entire building. Jean knew better than to walk through the flower garden that bordered the house—only the house servants and those having plantation business with Monsieur or Madam could go there—but he could not help peering through the dimness of the verandah as he passed, wondering if Monsieur was in there somewhere, or he if was still . . .

Jean shook his head.

Past the Big House, he followed a mud path back into the forest—a wilder and less cultivated cluster of mango and breadfruit trees, interspersed with shrubs and bushes. The slave quarters were nestled in a clearing, well-hidden from the sight of the Big House. The buildings were constructed from coral blocks, roughly thatched and whitewashed, and arranged in rows. Strips of blankets or sheets hung over low doorways and tiny windows. On the flat-beaten earth outside their doorways, women squatted beside charcoal braziers, brewing tea over their smoky flames, while their babies sat on the bare earth and toddlers ran around the clearing, yelling and tormenting mangy dogs with sticks.

Jean's footstep slowed almost to a halt. His mother's brazier was unlit. His baby sisters were playing stones by themselves by the doorway. Jean's heart was loose and painful as it kicked against his ribcage. His stomach was a nest of snakes. For the first time, despite his best efforts to delay, he had come home too soon.

Before Jean could turn to run back toward the plantation, Monsieur pushed aside the curtain and stepped out the doorway. He came out bent over, then straightened to his full height, smoothing back his wavy hair.

Immediately, the women stood, curtseyed, and issued a chorus of respectful greetings. "*Bonjour, Monsieur De Sagré.*"

The master adjusted his waistcoat, pulled out his gold pocket watch, frowned at the time, and pocketed it again. Then he saw Jean, and his expression changed, turning cool and amused as he considered the boy before him.

"There you are," he said. "Your mother is looking for you."

Jean said nothing, but something in his expression made the master tilt his head back, as if Jean had said something insolent.

"You should be more grateful, boy," he said. "I have always been generous to your mother. When your father died I could well have evicted her, but she lives here, rent free. She and your siblings continue to benefit from my generosity and my paternal care. You should learn to show a little gratitude."

Jean looked at him. The line of the master's lips hardened.

"Well?" he said. "What do you have to say?"

Jean looked at him. The attention of all the women was now

focused on the two of them.

"Everyone here is grateful," Monsieur said.

"*Oui, Monsieur*," the women said in ragged unison. "*Merci, Monsieur.*"

"Exactly," Monsieur said. "And they know how to show their gratitude. All I am asking for is simple thanks."

Jean just looked at him.

"Helene!" Monsieur shouted over his shoulder. Jean's mother ducked out of the doorway and stood just behind the master's shoulder. She kept her head and eyes lowered, and something molten and burning welled up inside Jean.

His clenched his fists. *Silent Jean*, he thought. *I am Silent Jean.*

Monsieur spoke without breaking eye contact with Jean. "Helene, tell your little bastard how grateful he should be."

"He is very grateful, Monsieur, we all are . . ."

"I want to hear it from him!"

Jean's mother raised her eyes and looked at him. "Say thank you to Monsieur, Jean. He has been very kind to us."

Jean shifted on his feet. He was shaking. For the first time, he broke eye contact with the master, and looked down. A stone rested by his feet—one of the few remaining on the smooth patch of sand, probably because it was too large for the little ones to handle. It was the size of a mango, except dark.

Its darkness appealed to him . . .

"Jean," his mother repeated. "You need to show Monsieur some respect."

Jean raised his head, his eyes burning. "How can you?" he whispered. He pointed at the master. "With *him*?"

"I knew it!" Monsieur said. "The moment he speaks, insolence!"

"Jean De Sagré!" his mother said. "You will apologize and

thank Monsieur for his kindness, or I will give you a switching!"

"No!" Monsieur said. "I will personally whip the skin off his back!"

Inside Jean, everything gave way, and the molten fire erupted. He bent and grabbed the stone. It might have been too big for the other children, but not for him. In one movement, he rose and whipped it at the master's face. The stone struck the bridge of Monsieur's nose with a wet crunching sound. With a grunt, the man fell back, his feet folding under him. Jean's mother stood with her eyes wide and mouth open for an instant before the screams rose from her throat. She fell on her knees before the inert body.

His mother's grief only maddened Jean. He had barely been able to stop himself from picking up the stone and throwing it again—this time at her. Instead, he had raced out of the clearing and down the slope. The bushes whipped him, thorns tore his skin. Behind him, the screams and commotion had intensified, but Jean pounded on. The forest gave way to the mangrove swamps. He struggled through the mud, piercing his feet on their vertical roots and shells, until he reached the meeting of the swamp and the sea.

Blind to the expanse of water, milky blue under the morning sun, Jean collapsed, panting and sobbing, his hands and knees sunk deep into the mud. He could no longer hear the voices behind him. All that remained was the sound of waves far out at the reef and, as the eruption within cooled, the wind moaning.

A shadow had fallen over him. He looked up. The man had been pale, tall, and bald. He dressed almost as well as Monsieur did.

His eyes were curiously dead, like stones.

"Jean De Sagré," the man said. "My name is Geist. Are you

tired of living as a slave?"

Chapter Three

The mermaids swept out of the green haze five hours after Sartish and Jonah died. They had the fins of dolphins, seahorses, and even the tentacles of an octopus. Their human halves displayed every color or age, and they adorned themselves with an array of salvaged treasure from sunken shipwrecks, as well as conches and clamshells.

They circled, examining the pair of corpses with intent expressions.

Are they supposed to be here now?

I don't think so, but perhaps they forced their fate.

No. This is not their time.

How do you know?

I know. I have been doing this a long time. There was no storm. They are not wounded.

But they may have forced their fate.

Why don't we bring them back and ask them, just to be sure? If they forced their fate, we can take their breaths again.

A silence followed as they all considered this suggestion. Then,

Very wise. Astarshe and Khyro—you do it.

A gold-skinned mermaid with the tail of a red snapper and another with an elaborate pile of hair and the body of an eel obediently broke the circle and approached the bodies. Taking the heads of the dead young men in their hands, they leaned forward with an almost ritual slowness and kissed them on the lips.

Sartish's lungs convulsed. Water slipped past his lips, salty then cool and sweet in his mouth and throat like liquid air, its currents moving in his chest. He recalled the sensation from the last time the mermaids had brought him back. There was something comforting about it. He relaxed into the slow breaths and opened his eyes. Everything around him was clear and sharp, which heightened his relief at being alive again. Beside him, Jonah was also convulsing into life. Close by were two mermaids—one with sharp Asiatic features and gold skin, the other plump and cheerful-looking, with hair piled up. Sartish guessed that they were responsible for the kisses that had brought them back, while the rest continued to circle them, watching as if trying to decide whether to come closer.

Jonah's voice, full of joy, sounded inside Sartish's head, startling him. *I cannot thank you enough for bringing us back . . .*

A woman responded, light and full of laughter. *We weren't sure we should have.* No one's lips moved, but from the way the plump mermaid smiled, Sartish was sure she had spoken. As if provoked, one of the circling mermaids broke ranks and swam forward. She had curly white hair and the tail of a giant seahorse.

I am Ruzhivo, Queen of the Eastern Sea. Why did you put us to the test?

Jonah bowed his head and spread his arms. *Forgive me, Your Highness. These are unusual circumstances. We need your help.*

Really. Unusual enough for me to wake you and break our most sacred law?

I believe so.

Tell me. I will decide.

Jonah told their story again. Ruzhivo looked back and forth between him and Sartish. *You want us to wake Bas Rabyah.*

Jonah nodded once. *He is the only one who can help us to liberate our People.*

A long silence followed. The sea around Sartish shifted and breathed, playing over his skin. Beyond the circle of mermaids, faint beams of sunlight lit up clouds of plankton in the currents.

Finally, the Queen spoke. *Do you know our purpose here?*

There was silence, but Sartish could see a cloud of anxiety touching Jonah's face.

Ruzhivo continued in measured tones. *In the beginning, the Angeli chose air, the Djinn chose fire, the Blind Watchmen chose earth. And we chose water as our Element. The Wind gave each of us a purpose. The Angeli bear witness, the Blind Watchmen protect the borders. Our purpose is to keep the dead until the Higher Mysterion.* *Only when we know that someone does not belong among the dead have we returned them to the surface. My sister Cybele woke that girl Isabella—* She turned to Sartish, her gaze unnervingly direct. *And you as well, Sartish Kutty.*

Sartish bowed his entire body and spoke in his mind, remembering how to do it. *I am grateful to you, Your Highness.*

Queen Ruzhivo nodded and turned back to Jonah. *But you will understand why it is we cannot make a habit of bringing back the dead any time someone needs a little assistance. That is not our purpose.*

These are different circumstances, Your Highness.

They always are.

The pirates cannot prevail against the People of the Wind, the Elder's People. Not after everything he sacrificed.

Sartish could hear the desperation in Jonah's voice. Why couldn't he just accept that this wasn't the way? Maybe the Queen would send them back to the surface, which wouldn't be so disastrous, in Sartish's estimation. They could get back to the Island and use the Lamp to destroy those scum once and for all.

Have you considered the kind of help you are seeking? Ruzhivo said, frowning. *Are you aware that the Mezoramians do not see Mysterion quite as we do? Your allies may prove more troublesome than your enemies.*

I have considered it. Jonah sounded as if he wished she hadn't asked. *And I have to allow a . . . a certain ambiguity.*

Queen Ruzhivo glanced at the other mermaids and for the first time, Sartish sensed that she was uncertain.

Very well, she said at last, sounding tired. *You are appointed of the Wind and you will bear the burden of our choices.*

Jonah bowed again with evident relief. *I trust that the Wind will blow us where It will.*

We will have to bind you for the journey. It will not be pleasant.

Jonah looked at Sartish. Sartish wanted to argue, but something in Jonah's eyes told him it was no use. He had made up his mind. Sartish could only hope that the Mezoramians were as warlike as the stories said.

Sartish nodded, and Jonah turned back to Ruzhivo. *We understand.*

Ruzhivo gestured at the mermaids. They closed in around Sartish and Jonah. The golden-skinned one pulled Sartish's arms down to his sides. Sartish tried to raise them again, but they were now stuck in place. He kicked, but his legs had become paralyzed. His neck had stiffened too, his body floating sideways until it was horizontal. Fight and struggle as he might, he could do nothing to right himself.

Sartish screamed his frustration. No sound came out, but the mermaid beside him flinched a little and shook her head.

Best not to worry yourself. We bind everyone who travels with us.

I know! Sartish shouted. *And I hated it the last time, too!*

Jonah too floated on his side, hands by his sides.

We're in this together, Jonah said. *Try not to panic.*

I am not panicking, Sartish said. *All I can say is, I hope you are right about all this!*

They were on the move, the mermaids finning in formation around them. Sartish and Jonah kept up without effort, impelled by an invisible force. They accelerated, and Sartish's frustration soon gave way to paralyzing terror as they rushed at a dizzying speed through seaweed forests and coral formations, over plains littered with boulders, and through great multicolored shoals of fish that parted before and closed behind them like living curtains. After hours of water streaming over his face, exhausted from the intensity of the journey, Sartish's eyes drooped. He fell asleep, and for once it was pure and free of the nightmare—just a darkness through which wind blew like an endless breath. When he opened eyes—minutes or days later, he couldn't tell—it was dark, and they were still moving.

Jonah—Elder Jonah—are you there?

Jonah's voice sounded drowsy. *I'm here, Sartish.*

Do you know where we are?

No.

One of the mermaids spoke. *We are near.*

Sartish could feel it now. The water running over his skin slowed, and the curtains of water around him turned from impenetrable black to blue. He still could not discern any shapes around them, even the mermaids.

The voice of Ruzhivo floated in. *We are here.*

Where is here? Sartish said.

My apologies. Our eyes are used to the darkness.

A flame flickered to life—a strange, liquid fire held up by one of the mermaids—and then another, and another.

Sartish's heart slowed.

They were in a vast, low-hanging cavern. Far away at one end the water was now a distinct shade of blue—the entrance, where the first rays of light were beginning to feel their tentative way from the surface.

As far as he could see—the mermaids' lights could not penetrate its furthest recesses—the cavern around him was filled with an uncountable multitude of bodies, all of them wrapped in familiar strips of cloth, each held suspended in place with ropes that hung from the ceiling and rose from the floor.

Even in his own thoughts he could barely bring himself to say it. *The dead . . .*

The Queen spoke. *The sleepers. Until the Higher Mysterion.*

Beside him, Sartish could feel Jonah's silence.

How many are there?

Many, from all time until now.

A thought came to Sartish, and he spoke before he could stop himself. *What about those who were given to the sharks?*

Queen Ruzhivo paused before answering. *I am sorry, we do not know about those ones. Come now, Bas Rabyah is down there.*

The mermaids weaved among the bodies without touching them, deeper into the cave. The undersea torches they carried played in watery patterns over the uneven surface of the roof. Sartish and Jonah followed their guides, impelled forward by the same invisible force that had carried them here. Occasionally, their limbs brushed against one of the bodies, and Sartish shivered at the horror of the touch. Despite the flames, the darkness weighed more and more on them as they went deeper into the place of the sleepers—rows stacked on rows. Light caught the white grave cloths, then dropped them into darkness.

As they went deeper into the place of the sleepers, Sartish's mind thrashed around in a panic, but he dared not speak his thoughts. The desire to scream overtook him. He no longer cared. Nothing was worth this . . .

Then they stopped.

The mermaids had gathered around a body. The flames of their torches played on the creviced wall—the end of the cave. Queen Ruzhivo was beckoning them closer and gesturing toward the body.

This is the one.

They looked down at the body in silence. It was small, like that of a child.

He was the Elder's companion, Jonah said. *They were inseparable during his quest to fashion the Lamp.*

Sensing Jonah's disappointment, Sartish said: *It is not too late to go back.*

Jonah took a deep breath. *No. We're here, and we must follow this path to the end.* He nodded to Ruzhivo. *Your Highness.*

The mermaid held his gaze, as if making sure. Then she sighed, bent, and unwrapped the bandages, revealing an old man with a sharp, shriveled face in a single long garment, his arms folded across his breast.

The mermaid Queen nodded to the others. In perfect unison, the mermaids started singing together. Some of them intoned an almost discordant, wordless melody, while the rest droned a single-note bass line. The whole song filled and echoed through Sartish's head, leaving no room for thought or feeling.

After several minutes, the song faded. In the silence that followed, as if performing some ancient ritual, Ruzhivo bent and kissed the Wandering Sailor on the mouth. He started awake, thrashing and knocking the mermaid Queen backwards as he floated into an upright position, blinking and staring around.

Bas Rabyah was panting in slow motion, as someone does when breathing water, and his thoughts invaded Sartish's head—a strange mixture of familiar and unknown words, spoken in a high, terrified voice.

We are done, Ruzhivo interrupted the Sailor's confusion. *And now you must leave and never ask this of us again.*

We will not disturb you again, Jonah replied. He added with a smile, *Other than to bring us to rest here in the proper time.*

Of course. Ruzhivo inclined her head. *That is our purpose.* She gestured to her retinue, who led them out. At first, the Wandering Sailor struggled, knocking several of the bodies as they passed, but the mermaid Queen said something to him that was somehow both soothing and commanding, and the old man relaxed.

They emerged from the darkness. Sunbeams pierced down through the water from above. Sartish realized that the cavern was the underside of an underwater island, complete with white sand beaches, vegetation, and coconut trees whose palms swayed back and forth in the ocean currents. Swimming about the island, hundreds of mermaids paused to watch them in silence as they rose toward the surface.

We have no boats, Ruzhivo said. *You will have to go on from here alone.*

Sartish wondered whether Jonah had thought of that. Then he saw bright shapes flickering above the surface.

The Angeli have come for us, Jonah said. He sounded both surprised and pleased.

How did they know? Sartish asked.

They must have been watching our progress from the top of Mysterion.

Very well, Ruzhivo said. *We will leave you now. Farewell.*

I cannot express my gratitude . . . Jonah said. But the rest of his words were lost as Sartish broke the surface. A pair of feathery hands lifted him to the air, coughing and spewing water from his mouth and nose. He took a breath, and air burned his lungs. Azrel's voice spoke in his ear, familiar in its sarcasm.

"Wonderful. First I have to drag you around in a boat, and now I have to carry you on my back! Not much use, are you?"

Sartish tried to reply, but nothing but a croak came out.

"At a loss for words too, I see," Azrel said. "Well, I will consider it a gift. I'm sure you'll be flapping your mouth in no time." In one movement, without visible effort, the Angelus tossed Sartish onto her back.

"Ugh." She shuddered. "Why any self-respecting Elemental would ever choose to live in water is quite beyond me!"

Sartish said nothing, grateful for the bright warmth of her feathers. He would never tell her how happy he was to see her.

Below, two other Angeli were rising from the surface with Jonah and Bas Rabyah on their backs. Whatever Ruzhivo had said to the old man to calm him down had now worn off. He was catatonic with fear.

"Meet Uhrizel and Shantiel." Azrel introduced her companions. "Shantiel is a friend. She volunteered with me when the

Wind called us. Uhrizel didn't volunteer. He was sent along to make sure I don't interfere . . ."

Shantiel smiled at the comment. Uhrizel merely grimaced.

"Interfere?" Jonah croaked. "You?"

"Believe me," Azrel said, "if you met the Angeli, you'd know that I'm your biggest fan."

"Oh, you love it," Jonah said. "You'd be bored doing nothing but watching us all the time. Now, if you don't mind . . ."

"Yes, yes," Azrel said. "We're off to Mezoramia, I suppose."

Jonah looked surprised. "How did you—"

"We saw it all from our little perch above Okean," Azrel said. "I guessed that if Tala sent you to the Sleepers, you were looking for him . . ." She looked over at the old man, whose paralysis had rendered him deaf.

"You *must* have been bored," Sartish said.

"Oh, it didn't take me long to figure it all out," Azrel replied. "The question is, what happens when we get there?"

Jonah shrugged again. "No idea."

Azrel cocked her head at him. "Really? You don't know where you're going, so you brought a dead man back to life in the hopes he could tell you. And if he does tell you—which is in serious doubt at this moment—you *still* don't know what you're going to do when you get there. Have I got it right?"

Jonah rocked his head and smiled with a touch of weariness. "Pretty much."

"And you are surprised by this?" Sartish said to Azrel.

"Not really." Azrel shook her head. "I always knew he was crazy. But I have to say, this is the mother of all crazy."

Disagree

When the Djinn Overlords sent word that the young black boy was ready, Captain Hodoul personally went to collect him.

This was his usual custom. He didn't waste his time on adults, sending one of his least untrustworthy men to retrieve them. But since the Overlords rarely brought children from the lower world, and those taken from the Tree could produce no children of their own, the appearance of a child was a rare event. The Captain personally took responsibility for them. For months after their arrival, he gave them sanctuary in his mansion, tending to them until they had regained the strength that the Tree had drained from them. When he finally turned them loose to fend for themselves on the island, it was well understood that they remained under his protection. So they formed a little crew in their own right, stealing from everyone, torturing animals, and vandalizing houses—and no one could do a thing about it. If they were caught, the worst punishment the Captain would permit was a switching with the spine of a coconut frond. On more than one occasion, he had appeared as if out of nowhere to intervene in a beating that had gone beyond the limit that he had established.

Some of the Brethren complained. The Captain was too protective. There was something almost *personal* in his retribution against those who taught the little brats the lessons they deserved. But in the end, most of them agreed that Hodoul's actions were rooted in genuine self-interest, a desire to win gratitude and lifelong loyalty from his future servants while they were at their most susceptible.

When the Captain sent him from the mansion, the boy, who called himself Disagree, made up from the shreds of memory he had somehow held on to, had tried to join the children's crew in their games and nightly raids. Intimidated by his size and taciturn nature, they shunned him. Even at eleven, he was as tall as most adults, and almost as wide, and he spoke in single words. They left him out of their games because no one wanted him on their side. When they saw him coming, they ran away, and even when they were forced to sit beside him at the table reserved for the children during the Captain's monthly banquets, they simply ignored him and talked amongst themselves.

Things came to a head when Captain intervened. It was not unusual for him to join the children during one of their games. When he did, they dared not run from him, but sat with a terrified attention as he gave them an impromptu lesson in tying figure-of-eights and hangman's knots, or demonstrated cuts and thrusts and parries with his rapier, or told them stories of sea battles from his youth. Noticing the tall, silent child outside the circle of attentive faces, the Captain chose him as a fencing partner or called on him to tie the knot. But in the end, that had only made things worse. The children invented a new game, hunting him through the forest until they surrounded him, chanting, "Disagree! Disagree!" Still, none of them dared actually touch him. The stones he hurled to keep them back never failed to hit, leaving welts. Eventually, the children gave up and left him alone.

Disagree found a cave above the main camp, where he spent his days alone. From this height he could see the steep-pitched, thatched roof of the Captain's mansion at the edge of the bay. Sometimes he recalled the time he had spent there after the Tree, in the room decorated with old swords and maps. The Captain had brought trays of fish soup, pausing at the bedside to feel Disagree's forehead. He spoke little, other than to issue basic instructions: "Finish all your food." "There's hot water in that basin, clean yourself up." "Put your dirty clothes in that basket, and I will have them washed." Despite the brusqueness of the Captain's manner, Disagree could not remember anyone who had cared for him with such singular attention, even when he searched through the fog of his memories before the Tree.

He knew it was futile to hope that he could return to the mansion. Perhaps one day (as it was rumored) the Captain would choose an heir from among the children. But what were the chances he would choose Disagree, the boy who had exiled himself and would not even attend the banquets anymore?

Disagree's solitude came to an end early one morning, when a group of the oldest boys ambushed him outside the cave when he returned from raiding supplies. He did not see them as he pushed his way up the hill through the scrub, bent over under the weight of a gunny sack heavy with several large legs of dried salted pork, a bag of sugar, and a few utensils to add to his collection, including a frying pan.

Knowing he was close to the cave, Disagree looked up. Only then did he notice shapes shifting among the boulders, just before they raced out to encircle him—six of those almost old enough to join the adult gangs. He could not see their faces in the pre-dawn dimness, but he recognized the leader—Sharkey, as he liked to call himself—from the distinctive way he lifted his right foot higher than the left.

Disagree dropped the gunny sack and picked up a stone. He could tell from their faces that they weren't going to hold back this time. He might take out one or two, but the rest would keep coming. This time, they would get him.

"So that's it, boys." Sharkey's high, rather hoarse voice lingered on the final consonants of every word. "It wasn't a rat getting to the loot before we did." He stepped closer, just out of reach of Disagree's arms. He was no fool. "It wasn't a rat. It was worse than a rat. It was a thief stealing from his Brethren."

Disagree knew what was coming. He had seen it twice in the past month. It was the Code, and it applied to everyone.

"You cannot," Disagree said. He could hear the trembling in his own voice. "Not without the Captain's permission."

Sharkey's grin was wide and fixed now, his eyes hidden in the pits of his sockets. "I don't need permission," he said. "The Code is for adults, but we can do what we want. Next week I am eighteen, and I won't be able to touch you—" his lips twisted, "but not today. And when we're done, you can feed the sharks!"

One of the boys snickered. "Yeah, man!"

"Just try and take me," Disagree said, trying to sound more confident than he felt.

Sharkey seemed to guess his doubts. "You can't hold all of us off, thief. We are Brethren together. You are nothing!"

The boys had closed in their circle, but they were still outside of Disagree's reach. In the growing light, he could make out their intent, hungry expressions. They had watched the adults do this. Now it was their turn.

"Jump him!" Sharkey shouted. Then they were on him.

He shook, whipped them around, but they clung like giant crabs, nails digging into his flesh. One of them bit into his shoulder. Disagree yelled and dropped sideways to land with all his weight on the attacker. Something crunched under him. The boy screamed and let go. With one arm now free, Disagree punched out at the others. Their hold on him began to loosen, and Disagree struggled to his feet. Someone grabbed Disagree's free arm and pressed something against his throat. It stung, and the liquid of his blood trickled down his bare chest. Sharkey spoke in his ear. "You want to die a coward as well as a thief?"

Disagree stopped struggling. Around him the boys panted like dogs after a hunt. At his feet, one of them lay moaning.

"Tie his hands," Sharkey said. He shoved Disagree's right arm behind him. His arms were grabbed and pulled back as a loop of coir fiber rope slipped around his wrists, biting into his flesh. The noose slipped over his head and tightened. Sharkey strutted around behind him and pulled on the rope until Disagree started to choke and cough. "Now," Sharkey said. "Let's take a walk."

They drove him back down the slope, the air pink with the light from the east. Once Sharkey kicked the back of his knees, and Disagree stumbled and went over into the scrub. They dragged him to his feet by his neck, and he went on, following the path down back into the trees. Several minutes later, they stopped at the base of an immense breadfruit tree. A few rosy fingers of light descended from above.

"Take the rope up," Sharkey said to one of the boys—a scrawny one who walked with a slight hunch like a crab. The boy stared at Sharkey, as if he could not believe the big man had spoken to him, then giggled and ran to the tree. With the rope around his waist, he shimmied upwards with an agility that commanded awed silence from the onlookers, even Sharkey. Seconds later he had reached the lower branches, and Sharkey gestured—that was good, far enough. The boy hauled the rope, paying out the other end over the branch until it touched the ground. As the knot rose behind Disagree's neck, he saw those men and women dancing at the end of the rope. His legs trembled.

The others must have felt it too. Confronted with the reality of a hanging, no one moved.

"What are you waiting for, you cowardly dogs?" Sharkey barked. "Get to it!"

"What about you?" one of the boys said. Disagree didn't recognize him, but he looked a likely candidate as a rival to Sharkey—short, wide, and muscular, with a face that seemed to fold inwards, and deep-set eyes.

"What did you say, Moray?"

"Aren't you going to do anything, or are you just going to keep your hands clean while you watch us do your dirty work?"

Sharkey stared at Moray for the length of two deep breaths, then grabbed the end of the rope and dropped down on it with all of his weight. The noose tightened and jerked Disagree upward, coughing, though Sharkey's weight was not enough to pull him even onto his toes. Not to be outdone, Moray added his weight, dragging Disagree onto his tiptoes. Overcome with terror, Disagree struggled against his bonds. He thrashed against the rope with his body but succeeded only in tightening the noose further. At the other end, Moray and Sharkey were laughing—coarse laughter, void of pity.

Disagree cawed, no longer able to speak.

"Come on, you cowards!" Sharkey cried to the others. "What are you waiting for?"

"Get over here!" Moray said. "We're all in this together!"

Abandoning their last inhibitions, the others ran forward, snickering with terrified hysteria. They hauled Disagree into the air as he kicked and jerked and swung. The branch above, thick as it was, sagged and creaked. Shifting under his struggles and the uncoordinated efforts of his executioners, the noose's knot worked its way around under Disagree's chin, forcing his head backwards. As his neck creaked with agonizing intensity, panic overwhelmed him. He screamed, but the sound emerged as little more than a strangled croak. Darkness rushed in from the edges of his vision, obscuring the morning sunlight on the upper edges of the breadfruit tree. His lungs heaved in once more, then he relaxed, sinking away into himself, as the fight to breathe ended.

I die at dawn, he thought.

From somewhere at the far end of a roaring tunnel in his head, he heard a muffled explosion. He fell—though he was not sure whether it was in his head or in real life—and then his feet hit the ground and he collapsed on his side. At first, he felt no pain, but almost once, the need to breathe took hold of him. He fought against his bonds, twisted his head to loosen the knot, consumed with desperation. His lungs spasmed with the urgency to live, and at last, air trickled in—a thin, slow stream that seemed to work its way through a tunnel of fire in his throat. Yelling nearby, and *hiss-and-thwack*. Then the voices faded away, and someone jerked the noose off him and cut the rope that bound his hands. The sweet morning air flooded his lungs. Disagree coughed as the pain that he had never been so glad to feel—in his torn wrists, the muscles of his arms, the side of his head where he had landed, his throat and neck—the pain of being alive erupted at last. Overcome with the joy of it,

Disagree curled up and sobbed for the first time in many years.

Someone bent over him, blocking out the sunlight. Disagree turned his head as much as his aching neck would allow. He could not see the man's features, but from the untidy hair—glinting grey and silver at the edges—he could imagine the face, its features weathered and cracked with premature age.

"Monsieur Disagree," Captain Hodoul said. "You owe me a life of service."

"Yes, Captain," Disagree whispered, the effort to speak tearing in his throat.

The next day, he moved his belongings out of the cave and into the servant's quarters of the Captain's mansion.

Chapter Four

or days, the Angeli bore the three companions high above the expanse of Mysterion's ocean. Over the water below played every conceivable color, from the blinding gold and red of sunset, to green and blue dotted with the white specks of cresting waves. On some days, the surface darkened as clouds floated overhead. The rain thundered down and the wind ruffled the surface. On others, the ocean was a vast mirror reflecting the cormorants and frigates circling and diving, the high streams of cirrus above them, and the distant flickering shapes of the three Angeli arcing overhead like meteors.

In the course of the journey, they did not descend to land, even once. As Elementals of air, Angeli require no food or drink. When their passengers complained, they exchanged glances of amusement before passing back tiny flasks that contained a clear liquid, which Sartish recognized at once as water-from-above-the-heavens. After a single sip, their thirst and hunger vanished—for another day at least.

In the end, even the magnificent panorama of ocean and sky started to pall. Sartish attempted to occupy himself by engaging Azrel in discussions on every conceivable topic, from the taste of mangoes to abstruse questions on the nature of truth. Azrel was always game, but she tended to argue the exact opposite of whatever opinion he voiced, so that every discussion turned into a debate, which Sartish always lost, even if he was right. Soon he gave up on the Angelus and fell into a state of listlessness. His nights were restless, and the dream of Uncle Sat and the cigarette returned. Sometimes Sartish started awake, thinking he had heard the voice that had spoken into his ear on Qatala's shell.

He brooded over the words, *Do you really trust him?* It now seemed less a genuine question than a warning, as if whoever had spoken to him that morning had known something about Jonah. The New Elder's decision not to return to Elder's Island, but to seek help instead from Bas Rabyah, had only confirmed Sartish's feeling that someone was watching them, someone with alternatives to offer . . . Not for the first time, Sartish wondered who owned that voice. He could only conclude that it was a Djinn—only they could conceal themselves and speak out of thin air. If so, he definitely could not trust those words.

But still . . . Sartish glanced across at Jonah. They hadn't spoken much in the past few days, Jonah immersed in the daydreaming state Sartish had come to know so well. And when Sartish did try to get a sense of how they would proceed when they reached Mezoramia, Jonah shrugged and said something about listening to the Wind or trusting the Wind or hoping the Wind was blowing the right way.

"What does that mean?" Sartish cried, raising his eyes heavenward in frustration.

"It means I don't know," Jonah replied. "But I am willing to allow whatever happens to be what it is going to be."

The conversations had ended there. And now Jonah was lost in reflection again, staring beyond the horizon. Despite his apparent absence, he rode Uhrizel hands free, holding on with his knees. Something about that reminded Sartish that despite everything, Jonah was as capable a leader as he had ever seen. He often talked vaguely, but when it came time to act, he did so with confidence and insight.

So, maybe he is right about this too, Sartish thought. Besides, how could he trust the voice of a Djinn over someone who had saved him from the Blind Watchman, with whom he had shared his own blood? Jonah deserved more than that. And perhaps the Mezoramians would rise to the occasion and ease his doubts—that is, if they demonstrated a little more boldness than the current representative of their race . . .

Sartish looked over at Bas Rabyah. The old man was clinging to Shantiel with the same desperation as when she had first pulled him from the water. He kept his eyes shut for most of the journey, and when he had occasionally ventured a peek, his face had turned grey, and he had hastily closed them again.

Oddly enough, Bas Rabyah's terror had not inhibited his mouth to the same degree as his eyes. Within the first hours of their flight, his silence had thawed into a torrential monologue that had flowed nonstop—with short breaks for sleep—ever since. It had begun when Jonah had explained their need. Bas Rabyah's eyes flew open just long to reveal his horror. "You wish me to return to that oasis of sorrow?"

Jonah spent two more days trying to persuade him of their case. Bas Rabyah countered his arguments with lengthy narratives that detailed everything from his earliest memories to the moment he had breathed his last, lying on the Elder's own bed while Aquille held his hand and wept for his departure.

"And then, to be woken from the sleepers," he said, shaking his head. "To be asked to go back to my beginning . . ."

At last, Jonah looked at Sartish with helplessness in his eyes.

He didn't foresee this, Sartish thought. He took a deep breath, and muttered, "Let me try." He turned to Bas Rabyah. "My Lord, I was once a servant of the Djinn, one of those who now besiege the Elder's Island."

Bas Rabyah had opened his eyes, paying attention now. Heartened, Sartish continued to tell of life among the Brethren—the raids and plundering, the whippings and hangings, the torture sessions in the basement of the king's mansion. When he mentioned how the Brethren did not bury their dead or send them to the Cavern of Sleepers with mermaids, but instead threw their bodies to the sharks, Bas Rabyah's face had turned grey. Seeing that he had captivated the old man's sympathy, Sartish concluded his account with a morbid touch, "And the sharks leave nothing behind. Not even the bones."

"Then they have no hope," Bas Rabyah whispered, "in the Higher Mysterion?" He turned to Jonah with the question.

Jonah rocked his head. "We cannot say."

For the first time, Bas Rabyah fell silent, staring at the horizon.

"I have been given a second life," he said at last. "But the servants of the Djinn receive no such blessing." He turned back to Jonah and Sartish. "I will follow you as I followed the Elder before you. I will help you."

As Bas Rabyah had clasped their hands, sealing his oath, Jonah glanced at Sartish, gratitude transparent in his eyes. At the sight of it, a breath of relieved joy had swept through Sartish, a lightness than he hadn't felt in months. He inclined his head, acknowledging Jonah's thanks. Pride forbade him from showing more.

After that, Bas Rabyah had taken it upon himself to educate them about their destination. In a monologue that continued for another two days, he recounted every detail about Mezo-ramia—the interlocking glass blocks of its outer wall, shaped in the form of a coracle so that the whole could float on the shifting sands; the peasant slums, the merchant neighborhoods and bazaars, the green palm oases and fountains of the public parks; the inner circle, where the houses of the lesser nobles shoved to get as close as possible to the House of the Mighty One, resplendent in semi-transparent arches and pillars. And deep below them all, great pipes descended beneath the foundations and pumps drew water from deep under the sands, channeling the precious fluid to water the homes of rich and poor alike.

The day after that, Bas Rabyah had rhapsodized about the public markets where vendors sold the dried meat of giant serpents; exotic birds who could recite the entire history of Mezoramia on command; miniature tame water dragons who were content to live in bowls of water and entertain their owners with acrobatics; and of course, woven baskets that overflowed with the abundance of dates and figs and pomegranates and golden apples imported from the south in solar-sailed hover-ships that jetted in and out of the desert all day long, replenishing the city's supplies until sunset, when the gates were shut.

And now, Bas Rabyah was recounting how the merchant and lower classes would gather every evening in the public parks, while the Mighty One and his lesser nobles sat on their balconies, waiting for the cool of the night. Amateur musicians gathered into ensembles and played popular songs. Between sets, poets recited their latest compositions, and storytellers the latest instalments of their epics, until the stars came out and the moon rose and the air cooled enough that sleep became possible at last.

Sartish lifted his head and looked across at him. "You sound as if you are missing it."

Bas Rabyah paused in surprise, as if he didn't think anyone had been listening to him.

"It was indeed beautiful," he said.

"Then why were you leaving it?" Sartish asked. The truth was, he had been resenting the old man's enthusiasms.

"The Elder," Bas Rabyah replied. "He called me to a bigger world."

That night, the Angeli left the ocean behind, and the companions woke to an expanse of tawny-colored sand that rolled away in waves to the horizon. The sky was a hard blue, devoid of a cloud that might have offered respite from the sun, which poured fire down on them, sucking moisture from their skin. They drank almost every hour from the flasks of water-above-the-heavens, grateful that they never ran dry.

Bas Rabyah's torrent of a narrative finally dried up, and the companions huddled close against their Angeli, enduring the worst of the heat in silence until the sun set at last, an explosion of red and gold in their faces. Unlike the ocean, the air over the desert turned cold at night, freezing them as much as it had burned them during the day. Below, the dunes undulated pale and endless in the moonlight.

Sartish dreamed of Uncle Sat again, and when he woke, the sun had already launched its assault. He retreated into the darkness of his mind, where the doubts that he had pushed back had returned full strength. He brooded on the quest, which seemed more futile and unreasonable than ever. They had the most powerful weapon in the world waiting for them to wield it against their enemies, and here they were in the middle of nowhere, going who knows where, all because Jonah had some foolish ethical qualms about a horde of degenerates who wouldn't hesitate to cut them to pieces given the opportunity . . .

He was so embroiled in his thoughts that he didn't hear Azrel speak. Then Bas Rabyah shouted. Sartish raised his head. Like the sails of a great ship of the sands, the spires of Mezoramia rose above the horizon. With every passing hour, it climbed higher, more magnificent in reality than in their imaginations, its glass-stone blocks like sculpted water, shimmering and partially reflecting the brilliance of the sunlight.

As they circled overhead, soldiers in uniforms gleaming white and gold and carrying long-handled *shotels* ran back and forth with their heads craned upwards. The incoherent shouts of their commanders carried even to this altitude as they tried in vain to order their men back to their posts. Soon the consternation on the battlements spread down to the narrow streets, which teemed with crowds, mostly clad in white. One by one, they noticed the flaming shapes that fluttered in circles above their city. The purposeful flow of traffic slowed to stop. Faces turned to the sky. Fingers pointed and faint cries rose up.

"So," Azrel said. "Where would you like us to drop you off?"

"Somewhere nearer the ground, if possible," Jonah replied.

Azrel rolled her eyes. "A little more specificity would be appreciated."

"You are not staying to protect us?" Bas Rabyah said, his eyes wide open and terrified.

Uhrizel spoke for the first time, his tone sharp. "No. We are forbidden to interfere."

Azrel sighed. "Unfortunately, that's the case. We'll find a spot to put you down, make sure you're safe—" she threw a defiant look at Uhrizel, as if daring him to argue. But he said nothing, and she continued, "And then we'll go back above-the-heavens. We will return when you need us, which I'm guessing won't be too long."

"Do not be too eager," Sartish retorted. "Someone might be thinking you need us more than we are needing you."

"I can't imagine anyone who would think that," Azrel said. "Besides, you definitely need us to get you to the ground."

"Not in the lower or middle city," Bas Rabyah said in a voice that trembled. "They will riot and tear us to pieces."

"How about the House of the Mighty One?" Jonah asked.

Bas Rabyah nodded and started to say something. A series of explosions interrupted him. Below, archers wielded recurved bows, aiming and firing. But instead of arrows, blue and white flames shot upwards, igniting only a few feet below them. Unperturbed, the Angeli rose well beyond range.

Bas Rabyah voice was faint. "Fire arrows . . ."

"Can you deflect them, Azrel?" Jonah said.

Azrel glanced at the other Angeli. A brief, silent exchange passed between them. Finally, Azrel nodded. "Yes," she said. "We'll shield you until we reach the ground, and then we'll draw their fire up with us."

"What then?" Sartish said. "How will we—"

"Hold on!" Azrel shouted, and dove toward the city, forcing him to grab at her. They plummeted toward the House of the Mighty One, its domes and spires swelling with alarming speed. A constant barrage of fire arrows rose up at them, exploding against the Angeli but somehow leaving them untouched. The domes flashed past. The pavement of the front courtyard rushed up at them. Just before they hit, Azrel fluttered and stopped so suddenly that Sartish felt his chest creak against her and his vision darken.

"Off!" Azrel said. Sartish slid off and collapsed on pavement. Nearby, Jonah and Bas Rabyah tumbled off Shantiel and Uhrizel. At once, the three Angeli rose up as the Mighty One's archers continued to launch fire-arrows at them. Distracted by the brilliance of those many-winged bodies, they forgot about the three companions who helped each other their feet, a little unsteady after so many days of flight.

"What now?" Sartish shouted over the detonations.

"Now we surrender," Jonah said.

"What?" Sartish said. "What do you mean, surrender?"

But Jonah was already kneeling, his hands above his head. Sartish followed suit. Only Bas Rabyah stayed where he was.

"Bas," Jonah said, "what are you doing? Kneel down!"

On the ramparts, men were shouting, pointing down at them. The Angeli's distraction had ceased to distract. As the archers turned, Bas Rabyah raised his hands. "I am Bas Rabyah, a citizen of Mezoramia! I claim the Absolute Right of Audience before the Mighty One, for myself and for those who walk with me!"

Sartish frowned in bewilderment. The old man had called out in another language, strange and guttural, with punctuating clicks. But Sartish had understood every word, as if he had known the language all his life.

Jonah had noticed his confusion. "It's one of the gifts that the Wind gave to the People of the Wind," he murmured. "We understand and speak all the languages of Mysterion, in the hope we can bring all together again."

Bas Rabyah had knelt beside Jonah again. On the ramparts, the archers were paralyzed, looking over at their commanders. The commanders were no less confused, gathered in a little group, arguing. At last, one barked a command and, without waiting for the order to be obeyed, hurried down a set of stone steps toward the courtyard. Several archers shouldered their bows, drew spears, and followed him down.

"Every Mezoramian has the right to see the Mighty One immediately upon request," Bas Rabyah said, "but only once in his lifetime. I have never used that right." He grinned, showing all of his teeth. "Until now."

Jonah was silent. "I cannot say how grateful we are."

"The Elder was my companion," Bas Rabyah said. "I would do anything for him. And for those he has chosen," he added.

The commander and his detachment of soldiers hustled them, manacled hand and foot, through the main doors of the House. The interior was vast and cool. From all around came the chuckling sound of running water, like a confluence of many streams. Looking around, Sartish could not identify the source of the sound until Bas Rabyah touched his shoulder and gestured down at the floor. The tiles underfoot were stone lattice laid over a maze of water channels. Bas Rabyah pointed out a series of ledges that spiraled in intricate patterns around the walls to windows in the top of the main dome.

"More streams," he muttered.

"They cool the house," Jonah said.

"Ingenious," Sartish murmured. Perhaps, he thought, Jonah had been right to throw their lot in with the Mezoramians after all.

Their guards marched them across a wide atrium within which stood a smaller walled enclosure. Men and women clustered in small groups around the room, all wearing ornamented white robes, their hair also white (Sartish was sure this was some kind of dye, since even the youngest wore stripes of white).

"Petitioners," Bas Rabyah murmured. "The nobles come first, the merchants after noon, and the peasants just before sunset."

As they entered, the petitioners' murmurs died. Heads craned to get a better view, or leaned together to whisper a snide comment. The guards did not pause, sweeping through another set of doors into the inner enclosure.

Here they stopped. Before them lay a pool of deep green water that roiled and rippled under the force of a current somewhere deep beneath. A series of flat circular pavestones led across the water to a glass-stone platform at the center of the pool, where the Mighty One—he could be no one else—sat on a low, ornately carved bench. Beside and slightly behind him stood a tall thin black man in a long silver robe, his bald head gleaming in the light from above. He tilted his head back when he saw the companions, and his distaste was evident, as if he could smell them even from where he stood.

By contrast, the Mighty One leaned forward to examine the new arrivals with fascination. He was a small middle-aged man, tending to scrawny, with golden brown skin. His pure white hair exploded untamed in every direction like flames, and his movements were quick, birdlike, and sudden. He also wore a silver robe, though his was decorated with intricate geometric patterns made of glass beads and crystals.

The commander made no attempt to cross to the island platform. He bowed low. "Mighty One Tasarakt, one of these strangers has invoked the Absolute Right of Audience on behalf of himself and those who walk with him."

"How do we know he can claim this right?" the tall man said in a petulant tone.

"My name is Bas Rabyah," Bas Rabyah said. "My father's

clan is Bastamy, who sought protection from the Lord and Father after the Great Battle and the flight to the west, but my mother was of the clan Meserekt."

The tall man looked startled. "She was one of the pure ones?"

"Yes," Bas Rabyah said. "But if you wish, my bloodline is recorded in the archives . . ."

The Mighty One's hands fluttered, and the tall man inclined his head reluctantly. "There is no need. You have your audience."

The commander stood aside and gestured to Bas Rabyah. The old man took one step forward and raised his hands as if in supplication. "I was a young man, still living in my father's house. He was a glassblower for your predecessor but one, Suliman the eighty-fifth Gergesekt, and I was destined to follow his path. I, on the other hand, longed to be an archer in the Mighty One's army. I practiced with the bow in secret whenever I could. I enrolled in every competition and won a few, hoping that the commanders who judged the competitions would notice my skills and conscript me against my father's wishes. One day, when I was practicing among the dunes, a stranger walked out of the desert. He came from the east, from the center of Mysterion where the horde of the Djinn ruled at that time—"

"It is common knowledge that they still rule the cesspool in the East," the tall man declared. "And that stranger, as our chroniclers tell it, was one of their minions. His heresies divided the people, and they cast him out!"

The Mighty One's head snapped around, birdlike. "Let him continue, Prime Minister. It is his right!"

The Prime Minister pursed his lips. The Mighty One's hand invited Bas Rabyah to continue.

"The stranger, his name was Aquille, was on a quest to make a Lamp that he said would cast out the Djinn once and for all. He required a glassblower to make the font at the heart of the Lamp. No one would help him, because he was a stranger, even as your Prime Minister says." Bas Rabyah threw a cold glance at the tall man. "Your predecessor even issued an edict forbidding anyone to offer assistance. But I took pity on him and made the font from the purest glass-stone, risking death to do so—"

"And you dare come here with your petition," the Prime Minister cried, "having defied the Mighty One's sacred edict—"

"Silence!" the Mighty One roared, in a voice too deep for his small frame. "If we were to treat every edict issued by every fool who has sat on this bench as 'sacred,' we would not be able to let out a fart in mixed company without fear of losing our heads. However," he added, fixing the Prime Minister with his bright eyes, "if you should see fit to interrupt one more time the lawful utterance of a citizen's petition, I will issue an edict of my own that you will not enjoy. Do you understand, Prime Minister?"

"Forgive me, Mighty One." The Prime Minister pursed his lips, pressed his hands together and stepped backwards.

Sartish stared at Tasarakt. *Now* that's *a leader*, he thought. *That is what we need. None of this 'if the Wind blows' stuff!*

The Mighty One turned back to them. "Please, go on."

Bas Rabyah went on. "My defiance of the edict was soon discovered, however, and we both escaped the City with our lives. Aside from the clothes on my back and a few supplies to keep us alive in the desert, I took only a bow—one of my prizes I won at competition. And I am glad I did. I used it many times in the years that followed. Time will not permit me to tell how often . . ." Bas Rabyah paused for a moment, recalling the adventures with a faint smile. "After all those years, the Lamp was assembled, and I followed Aquille back to the center of Mysterion. There I witnessed his victory over the Djinn. I saw him blow a fire of wind from the Lamp, and they were driven before him and imprisoned in their own enchantment. By then, I had pledged my life to him, and I never returned to the Floating City. I buried my bow in the forest at the top of the Aquille's island, because after seeing the Lamp, I knew I would never use it again. I died years later, as contented as a man can be—"

"You died?" the Mighty One exclaimed. "What do you mean?"

Bas nodded. "I did indeed go down to darkness in the time the Light sets out for all of us. But I was awakened. This young man, Jonah, inherited the mantle of Aquille. He came to my resting place, called me back to life, and asked my help in the name of my old companion. He told me that the Djinn, though imprisoned, have continued to raise up those who were once their servants and yoke them into their abominable service again. These brigands have surrounded the People whom Aquille once gave so much to free, and now Jonah seeks help from Mezoramia to rid his world of their enemies."

Bas Rabyah fell silent, lowered his hands, and stepped back. His shoulders slumped, as if the effort of telling the story had cost him. Jonah touched his shoulder. Sartish wanted to imitate Jonah's gesture—the old man's account had filled him with a new sense of resolve—but he could not bring himself to raise his hand from his side before the moment passed. He hoped Bas Rabyah had seen the gratitude in his eyes.

The Mighty One leaned back, withdrawing into himself. Jonah and Sartish looked at one another, wondering what was next. Behind the Mighty One, the Prime Minister shifted from one foot to another, unsure what to do next. Finally, he took a tentative step forward, not quite level with the Mighty One's shoulder.

"Your Highness," he said, "there are many waiting . . ."

Tasarakt raised his head. "Indeed. I am ready to make my ruling." He directed his gaze at the three companions.

Here it comes, Sartish thought. For the first time, he really wanted this. All his muscles had wound themselves tight.

"Our Lord and Father saved our nation from death and destruction at the hands of the Djinn and their servants. He led us into the desert, to this very spot," Tasarakt pointed to the floor, "and he divined water to sustain us. Using only water and sand and light, we became a glorious nation." He gestured around. "We trade with the races to the North and South. Sometimes we do battle with them. But in the end, we are secure. We have no need of anyone, no need to look back to a past of corruption and suffering." He fixed his eyes on Jonah. "You and your kind turned against us, colluded with the Djinn, divided the races, and exiled us in the four corners of the world. Now you seek our help?"

Sartish's felt a cold film of dismay spread over his skin. It wasn't supposed to go this way. He glanced at Jonah. *Say something!*

"The Djinn are our enemies as much as yours." Jonah said, the Mezoramian gutturals and clicks rolling off his tongue as if he had born to it. "I want to ensure that we never go back to those dark times."

"We *have* ensured it!" Tasarakt shouted. "Here, in this place! We do not need to concern ourselves with you! What are you to us? Our Lord and Father separated himself from your kind fifty generations ago, and now you would draw us back into your . . ." Tasarakt paused, his mouth twisting in disgust. "Your degeneracy."

Jonah's face flushed. On the platform, the Prime Minister was smiling with satisfaction.

"What now?" Sartish muttered at Jonah. "Are you not going to answer?"

Jonah looked at him. "I have nothing say."

"Really?" Sartish said, incredulous. "Where is the Wind—"

"If you alone made the petition," the Mighty One interrupted. "I would refuse and imprison you. However, this son of Mezoramia," he nodded at Bas Rabyah, "has told of strange wonders. He is living proof of your power over death. And he speaks of a Lamp whose power exceeds our powers. Our Lord and Father's prophecies refer also to something like it. *O Fire of Heaven,*" he quoted, "*flow through the portal . . .*"

"Mightiness." The Prime Minister frowned. "I do not see how that reference has anything to do with that so-called Lamp—"

Tasarakt pointed at Bas Rabyah. "He spoke of the portal! This Lamp that cast out the Djinn. That is the portal!"

The Prime Minister rocked his head. "But it is generally agreed that the portal is simply a reference to the City gates—"

"Agreement is not fact," the Mighty One cut in. "It is a general opinion! And even if this Lamp is not the portal, then what is the wind of fire? It is all-powerful, consuming everything that is darkness, leaving only light!" Without waiting for the Prime Minister to answer, Tasarakt stood. "Hear my decision," he said. "I will recommend to the Council that we send the assistance you require to free your people."

The Prime Minister began to wring his hands, but he knew better than to interrupt.

Sartish held his breath. Beside him, he knew Jonah was doing the same.

"In return," Tasarakt said, "you will submit yourself to Mezoramia as a vassal. You will kneel before this seat, with the whole council present, and swear allegiance to us. You will swear to use all your powers, including this Lamp, for the good of Mezoramia. Or you can face your fate alone. You have three days." He addressed the guards. "Take them to the guest quarters. And send in the next petitioner!"

Disagree

From the beginning of his apprenticeship, Disagree knew that the Captain kept secrets. At first, Hodoul had taught him little more than how to clean the mansion and cook the meals. Impressed at how quickly Disagree learned (and particularly at the quality of his cuisine), the Captain went a step further. After supper, he would retire to the verandah with a glass of palm wine and muse out loud about the past day, while Disagree waited by his rocking chair with a decanter, ready to refill his glass. The Captain never acknowledged these times as lessons, but it wasn't long before Disagree understood the complicated art of maintaining peace among the Brethren—whether it involved giving a bottle of the Captain's best wine in exchange for continued loyalty, seating someone closer to the head table at the banquets, or deciding between whether to fine, whip, or hang an offender who broke the Code.

But there were also things the Captain never spoke about. One night, Disagree heard the key turn in his door, locking him in, and voices outside, one of them pleading. The Captain issued a sharp command. There were several *thumps*, and then silence. The following evening, as he rocked and gazed out at the water, Hodoul murmured, "Leaders must sometimes do difficult, even extreme things, for the greater good. When those times come, we can never ask others to dirty their hands for us." He turned his eyes to Disagree. "When you are in my position, remember that."

Troubled, but not wanting to disappoint, Disagree nodded. "Yes, Captain." The next time he heard the key turn in his lock and the sounds of pleading from downstairs, he imagined standing beside the Captain, doing those difficult things, and the anxiety swept through his mind. His sleep was restless and full of nightmares.

He knows I am not ready, he consoled himself. *That's why he locks the door.*

The opportunity to prove himself came a few weeks after his fourteenth birthday. Captain Hodoul had summoned the captains of the other crews to an evening audience, and Disagree was present as usual to pour wine and serve food. Hodoul had ordered him to keep his mouth shut and his eyes and ears wide open. This seemed unnecessary to Disagree, but he took it as a sign of the meeting's significance.

It was a time of fragile peace. The Captain had asserted the right to rule on behalf of the Overlords and enforced his claim in a series of single combats—all of which ended with his rivals' bodies being thrown to the sharks. Following these victories, Hodoul established the Code, and the remaining captains had signed it in their own blood. Only the Claw-men, who hunted sea-going dragons and controlled the manufacture and distribution of Claw powder, remained as aloof as always on the northeast island. The rest of the Brethren had committed, at least in theory, to living in harmony.

But the hard-won unity always teetered on the edge, ready to collapse into anarchy. Almost every week, another desperate Claw-hungry crew forgot their commitment to the Code and raided another crew's supplies. To stave off a round of retaliations, the Captain held court and hanged the instigators in the square in front of his mansion. For a few days at least, order was restored, but in private, the Captain fumed. "What is the purpose of a rule if some feel it does not apply to them?"

As always, Disagree said nothing. But it didn't matter. The Captain knew the answer: as long as the Claw-men lived beyond the Code, the rest of the Brethren would always be tempted to think they could do the same. That was the reason for the audience: to convince the others that the purveyors of dragon's claw powder were the common source of their ills, to be wiped from the face of the earth.

After the captains had departed to their own camps, Hodoul questioned Disagree not only about what he had heard, but also the language of gestures and body movements that testified to his rivals' secret intentions.

"And?" the Captain asked. "Were they convinced?"

Disagree shook his head.

"Of course not," Hodoul said. "Ethical arguments mean nothing to them. In the end, they will only act when I give them the opportunity to enrich themselves. Which is what I am going to do tomorrow night."

"Then . . ." Disagree hesitated. Even when invited he could barely speak in the Captain's presence. "Why do you . . .?"

The Captain smiled. "Why didn't I get straight to the point? Because, my boy, they need to *believe* that they are acting for the right reasons, even if they are just serving themselves. That is just how people are."

A few nights later, at the end of a second, equally fruitless audience, the Captain sighed and rubbed his eyes. "Well, perhaps it is time we table this issue. It is indeed difficult .

. . After all, even if we did manage to destroy them and their corrupting influence once and for all, how would we manage their stockpiles of Claw? How would we divide it in ways that would be fair and avoid further conflict?"

And just as the Captain had said, the captains around the table straightened up and leaned forward, a light flaring up in their eyes. On the next moonless night, with no running lights to betray them, the ships of the Brethren launched together for the first time and set a course for the northeast island.

Although Disagree was by that time old enough to fight alongside the adults and take a full share of the prizes, the Captain ordered him to remain on board during the attack. "Any degenerate can swing a cutlass or fire a rifle," he said. "And you will have many opportunities to do so one day. For now, just watch how a thinking leader can channel a mindless rabble toward a greater destiny."

Disagree received the instruction with his customary silence.

"Don't worry," Hodoul added. "You will get your chance, when you are ready."

Disagree nodded. "Yes, Captain." He didn't want to admit, even to himself, how little disappointment he felt.

Disagree watched from the Captain's balcony as the fleet swung broadside to the bay of the Claw-men's stronghold, launching volleys of fiery cannonballs in great orange arcs into the darkness. He gripped the rail as they dropped anchor and launched the raiding parties, and the boats raced into the mouth of the bay, giving and receiving volleys of fire from the shore as they went. The cacophonous sounds and sights of the battle overwhelmed him, filled his mind—the blazing of houses, the screams of the women and the shouts of the men, the ring of steel and the sharp rattle of rifle-shot volleys.

Eventually, the din faded away. The crackling of burning buildings and a bank of smoke drifted toward Disagree across the water, stinging his nostrils with the familiar acrid stench of burning dragon's claw. In the relative quiet, his heart beat in his ears, and the railing under his palms was slick with sweat.

When the crews returned, the mood was ugly. In the confusion, the Claw-men's storehouses had taken directs hits from the cannons. They had salvaged less than a month's supply. The Captain's crew was in an even worse mood. They returned with a single captive—a short thickset man with a head that resembled that of a tortoise—dragging him on deck with a roughness born of frustration.

The Claw-man fixed the Captain with bright black eyes. "I am ready to feed the sharks."

"And I promise that I won't disappoint you, Zarastra," the Captain replied. "But first, I need your assistance."

Zarastra spat a thick gob of phlegm at the Captain.

"As you can see," Captain Hodoul continued, gesturing across the water to the burning camp. "My men have been deprived of their rightful prizes. They are unhappy . . ." The crew around them shouted their agreement. "And they require compensation. That is why your life has been preserved, for just such a circumstance. You will guide us to your hunting ground and help us restore what we have lost."

Zarastra stared at him, then laughed. "Maybe tomorrow," he said. "Or the next day."

"No," Captain Hodoul said. "You will take us whenever I wish."

"Go on wishing," Zarastra retorted.

Captain Hodoul smiled. "Take him to the brig," he said. "I will work on him." He turned to Disagree, who stood in his usual place close by his side. "You will go along with them. I will come below momentarily."

Disagree felt a sharp pang in his guts. The Captain had unlocked the door. Faced with the moment at last, Disagree could no longer deny the terror he felt. But despite himself, he just nodded at the Captain, and followed the men as they dragged Zarastra into the tiny brig and chained the Claw-man in the cage. As they left, one of them grinned at Disagree. "Hope your stomach's empty, my young friend!"

Bile rose in Disagree's throat. He clenched his jaw and swallowed hard, trying to push it down. In the heat of the tiny brig, sweat broke out on his forehead and ran down his face. In the cage, Zarastra was now regarding Disagree with his tortoise eyes. The light of the lamp overhead gleamed on his black skin.

"Boy," he said at last. "What is your name?"

"Disagree," Disagree muttered.

"Well, Disagree," Zarastra said. "Now you will see what kind of man your master is."

Before Disagree could answer, the door swung back. Captain Hodoul entered, a canvas rolled under one arm. He wore an apron, which should have made him ridiculous; yet it struck Disagree as ominous. He wanted to run out of the brig and slam the door behind him, but the fist that gripped his insides held him, locked his feet in place. He could only watch, the expression fixed on his face as the Captain unrolled the canvas on a small table in the corner, revealing an array of knives, pliers, and saws.

"I thought I might do you the courtesy of telling you the truth before we start," the Captain said, without looking up. Disagree realized that he was addressing the dragon hunter.

"So you understand why you will soon experience the worst pain of your life. You see, this has nothing to do with stealing your stock of dragon's claw. That was just what I needed to motivate my degenerate horde to stop killing each other and band together into something that does justice to their name. And even if they had managed to get everything you had, it would all be gone in a matter of months, and we'd be back to the beginning again. No, the truth is I came here for you, and you alone. Do you know why?"

Zarastra did not reply, and Hodoul continued. "I think you do. The Claw-men have hunted the dragons to near extinction. In fact, my sources tell me there's only one hunting ground left, and somehow you have discovered a way to hunt it and keep the supply of claws coming without killing the beasts . . ."

Hodoul selected a saw, examined it for a moment, put it down, and chose something that resembled a corkscrew. "A leader lives in reality. And reality is, everyone needs the illusion of escape. Without it, people get anxious. They start to think they are trapped, that maybe they need to throw off their shackles . .
.

"I need my men to be able to escape regularly, without killing each other, and without actually escaping. To accomplish that goal, I need to control the source and supply of dragon's claw powder. Simply, you are the only one who knows where the source is and how to sustain the supply indefinitely. That's why I came for you. And sooner or later, you will share with me everything you know."

Zarastra laughed again, but it sounded strained. He was staring at the corkscrew, the sweat shining on his forehead.

"Very well, then," the Captain said. He turned to Disagree. "Do not look away, Disagree. Do you understand?"

Disagree nodded. The Captain searched his face. Seeing nothing, he nodded and stepped forward with the corkscrew.

The Claw-man's scream pierced Disagree, as if the Captain was driving the instrument into his own flesh. As the Captain continued to work on the Claw-man with the other tools, Disagree never looked away. But soon he began to sway, his skull filled until it was overflowing with Zarastra's screams.

Then his stomach lurched, his gorge rose, and he retched without bending over, the vomit spilling down his bare chest.

The Captain stopped and turned to him, his eyes hidden in shadows. He was breathing heavily. "Why did you do that?"

"I don't know," Disagree said, his mouth full of the acrid taste. The smell filled the room. He was struggling to breathe.

"You've seen blood before," the Captain said. "You've seen men hanged, their entrails spilling out. Why now? Tell me!"

Disagree didn't want to answer, but he knew he had no choice. He had tried to be strong for the Captain. He had failed.

He took a deep breath. "They pay for what they do. He does nothing."

Hodoul stared at him, his eyes concealed in the shadows. He glanced back at Zarastra, who was twitching but quiet, then laid down a pair of pliers. He rinsed his hands at a washbasin prepared for him in the corner. Drying his hands on a towel, he turned back, and Disagree saw his expression for the first time.

"I was wrong about you," the Captain said. "I thought you would be the one."

"I will try harder for you," Disagree said. He could hear the desperation in his own voice.

Captain Hodoul shook his head. "I know an irredeemable character flaw when I see one." He pointed at the door. "Go to bed."

Disagree lay on the tiny cot in the nook beside the Captain's cabin, his knees drawn up to his chest, trying to crush the agony of his humiliation. As the enormity of his failure overtook him, he choked up, and tears filled his eyes. He clenched his jaw to prevent the slightest sound, in case the Captain heard. When exhaustion threatened to drag him under, he started awake, thinking he had heard a scream below.

Well before the dawn, he got the Captain's breakfast from the galley as usual, but the Captain wasn't in his cabin, and his bed had not been slept in. Disagree wondered if he was still down in the brig when he noticed the apron hanging from the wardrobe door. It was speckled and smeared with dried dark spots.

The movement of the hull changed, heeling. They were underway. Disagree left the tray on the table and hurried up on deck. Above, the mainsails unfurled as men worked the rigging. The foresails were already set, driving them forward. Around them, the rest of the fleet also weighed anchor as the sails bloomed white on their masts. The crews hurried about their business with a palpable excitement.

Disagree started up the ladder to the poop deck. The Captain, wearing a fresh shirt and breaches and looking no worse for his sleepless night, was consulting with the helmsman. Seeing Disagree, he looked up.

"Did you forget something, Monsieur Disagree?"

Disagree paused in his climb.

"Did you forget that crew require permission to come onto the officer's deck?"

Disagree was silent. For the first time, he allowed tears to fill his eyes. "Permission to come on deck, sir."

"Denied," Captain Hodoul replied. "You will report to the

Steward and serve as his mate from now on." He turned away and continued to issue instructions. "West by North-West. If his instructions were accurate, and I believe they are, we should reach the hunting grounds in five days, wind permitting . . ."

Disagree clambered down the ladder one rung at a time. His feet had turned into solid iron, dragging him down. He could feel the eyes of the men watching him. Since he had become Hodoul's apprentice, they had watched and talked behind his back, but the absolute confidence he felt in serving the Captain had made their envy seem trivial, almost laughable. Now that he had been cast out, they would never let him forget his failure.

As he descended below deck, a sudden apathy came over him. For the first time, he did not immediately obey one of the Captain's orders. Instead of reporting to the steward, he made his way aft to the brig, where a crewman scrubbed the deck on hands and knees. If there had been blood, it was gone now.

Despite the darkness that now enveloped him, Disagree thought about the old Claw-man with his black eyes. *He get his wish*, he thought. *He probably beg for it too, at the end* . . . He hoped that at the very least, the Captain had use a sharp knife to end things quickly before throwing Zarastra to the sharks.

Chapter Five

Jonah leaned against the wall of the balcony overlooking the Floating City on the Sands. The translucence of the glass-stone blocks beneath his feet—the ubiquitous building material of Mezoramia—gave the impression of standing on solid murky air. Below, officials and bureaucrats scurried up the mosaic-tiled paths toward the Mighty One's house for the first audience of the day. On either side, stacks of flat-roofed buildings dropped away like uneven steps toward the lower districts and the edge of the City, the narrow streets between them teeming with crowds. Their morning noise—a sustained roar punctuated by occasional cries—floated up to Jonah, who regarded it all with a troubled frown.

Last night, he had lain awake, finally rising just before the dawn. The rosy-gold beauty of sunrise shattering against the glass-stone of the City had done little to calm the dark tide that swept in and out of his mind, the same questions repeated over and over again, the answers never coming.

Somehow, he had known all along it would come to this stark choice—he just hadn't wanted to believe it. And the more he thought about the choice, the more impossible it was. The Elder—that kind, wise old man who had taught him how to breathe the endless breath of Wind and kindle the Lamp—had entrusted to him all those whom the Wind had raised from among the Lethes and restored to Mysterion. Ever since, Jonah had made a habit of listening to the Wind, depending on It for even the smallest decision. When he closed his eyes, he could hear Its breath flowing through him, and when he needed the words, the gestures, they had come to him as long as he listened.

How could he now entrust himself to a people whose religion explicitly rejected the power of the Wind? He, Sartish, and Bas Rabyah had attended the daily noon liturgies, as all guests were expected to do, gathering with the Mighty One, his officials, and his household at the inner courtyard around a concave cube of pure glass-stone. The worshipers had chanted and prayed until the sun reached its zenith, and light shattered and exploded outwards from the heart of the cube. It had reminded Jonah of the fire of the Lamp, but during one of his sermons, Tasarakt had closed that door.

"We do not follow the vagaries of the wind," he declared, his eyes fixed on the three companions at the back. "Its aerial spirits led our ancestors to wander in error and confusion. We serve the Light alone!"

Jonah had left the liturgy convinced that he would never submit to Tasarakt under any circumstances. And then a voice had spoken into his head. *Perhaps the Wind is working through the Mighty One without him knowing it. How can you know? How can you judge the movements of the Wind?* Jonah had found himself again confused, uncertain, wondering if submission might not be so wrong . . . After all, what was the alternative? If he refused, Tasarakt would expel him from the City. Assuming the Angeli found Jonah before he died of thirst in the desert, the best he could hope for was a return to the island to be reunited with the People. They would be overjoyed, of course, but what then? The Lamp would protect them from the Brethren. No one could touch them as long as it stood guard. But they could never leave, either. They would be prisoners on the plateau for the rest of their lives, watching as the invaders destroyed the island, preparing the way for the Djinn to find their way back into the heart of Mysterion and spread their contagion over the world once again.

Tasarakt had not made deliberation easy. The day after their audience, the Mighty One invited them to join him on a tour.

Jonah was inclined to refuse. "He's set his conditions. We're not obligated to accept his social invitations on top of it."

Sartish looked incredulous. "Really? You do not think he might be softening his stance if we humor him a little?"

"I'm afraid I must agree, my Elder," Bas Rabyah said. "The marketplace opinion is that the Mighty One's temper turns suddenly in either direction. He may withdraw his offer entirely if he feels he has been slighted."

So, they had joined the Mighty One on his personal litter. Borne by six massive guards, they had descended through a spiraling tunnel to a vast cavern beneath the City where a great pump worked by mules drove water up into bronze pipes that rose like vines toward the surface. That afternoon, they had boarded Tasarakt's personal hover ship—a large flat vessel whose metallic sails drew its power from the sun—and skimmed out over the dunes to the sand-mining ships, their kilns billowing smoke as workers shoveled in pure sand, while others tended the molds to contain the streams of liquid glass that spurted out. The following day, they observed military maneuvers, the archers somersaulting from ship to ship, firing at dummy targets on the sand as they flew through the air. And finally, they had returned to the City and toured the many gardens scattered throughout the Floating City, where the stacked beds of wheat and barley and flax meant that the Mezoramians could grow three times as much in half the space, enough for every family to sustain themselves, if they were careful in their husbandry.

As they went, Tasarakt had lectured them continuously on the history of Mezoramia and its achievements, a mind-numbing chronicle of the names of the great ones—noblemen and women, engineers, architects, magi, warriors, poets, musicians, doctors—who had all raised the City to its present glory.

"We have fashioned life from death," Tasarakt declared. "No one can equal us in that. And no one can resist our might."

Jonah nodded, but said nothing. He could find no words, and the Wind was silent.

"And what of yours?" Tasarakt said, tilting his head back. "How do they live?"

Jonah attempted to explain. He tried to describe the fisher-men who did not need to do anything but go out just beyond the reef and drop their nets, only to have the fish rise up in shoals to fill them to bursting. He tried to convey the abundance of the fruit trees that bore mangoes and bananas and golden-apples and breadfruit and coconuts all year around, so that all you had to do was reach up and pick one ripe whenever you needed it. He tried to explain how the People did not need to work, but never tired of gathering to sing and dance and eat and drink and tell stories. But even as he tried to find the words, they evaded him. He hesitated and stumbled and repeated himself. He knew that life was real, but in the face of Mezoramia's glories, it danced away from his grasp like a mirage. As his explanation faltered and failed, the skepticism in Tasarakt's eyes give way to open derision.

He laughed. "You do nothing but sit and wait for the fish to rise, and the fruit to fall. And yet you hesitate to share in *this*?"

Jonah raised his hand, as if supplicating. "I have been given a responsibility for my People . . ." Then, with a touch of appeal, "It is not an easy choice, Mighty One. I am grateful for your continuing patience."

"You have it," Tasarakt replied. "Until tomorrow."

* * *

Jonah sighed and straightened up, stretching. He turned away from the morning scene and pulled aside the woven rug that hung over the doorway. The interior was dark and quiet, kept that way by more rugs that covered the glass-stone walls.

Jonah dropped the rug back into place and returned to the balcony wall, the sadness taking hold again.

The past three days would have been more bearable if he hadn't felt so alone. After the first day, Bas Rabyah had asked the Mighty One permission to wander the City to reacquaint himself with his old haunts. Tasarakt had readily agreed, perhaps believing that nostalgia would win his former subject over. After that, Bas had vanished, creeping back to their quarters after the very last drinking stalls of the night market had shut down. There was a heaviness in the old man's step, a clatter as he knocked something over, and when he passed close, a faint breath of wine followed in his wake. He was still asleep when they woke to join the Mighty One on the second morning and was long gone when they came back. Last night, Bas had not returned at all, and Jonah had started to wonder if the old man didn't want to look him in the eyes and admit that he was returning to the life of his people . . .

Of course, that was understandable, and it wouldn't have weighed so much on Jonah if it hadn't been for Sartish. Since their return from the Falls, Jonah had sensed a watchfulness in him, a distancing . . . As they had toured the City, Jonah had been troubled by the way Sartish fixed his black eyes on the Mighty One, leaning forward during his lectures. More than once he interrupted Tasarakt to ask a question, to the irritated amusement of the Mighty One. The noonday liturgies and the Mighty One's sermons had so engrossed him that Jonah, eager to leave as soon as the last word of dismissal was uttered, had to touch his shoulder to bring him back from the place to which he had been transported. When the Mighty One had dismissed Jonah's account of the People's ways, Sartish had said nothing, but his eyes had echoed Tasarakt's scorn. Somehow that had made things worse.

But there was something more, something darker. The previous night, something had woken Jonah. The room was pitch black, the rugs on the walls and over the doors blanketing out any sound. After lying for a while, Jonah knew that sleep had deserted him. He decided to get some fresh air on the balcony.

As he pushed past the curtain and into the open air, the cold of the desert night—brilliant under a full array of stars and a nearly full moon—assaulted him. He shivered. The Mighty One's compound was quiet, the lawns and pathways and building draped with pale and shadowy light. From lower down in the City the occasional cry of an animal or a sleepless infant rose up, then faded, intensifying the silence.

Jonah looked over the balcony wall, and his breath caught in his throat. In the courtyard, Sartish stared down into one of the City's many drinking pools, its surfaced troubled from the current that fed into it from the underground pipe. From this angle, Jonah couldn't see what Sartish was looking at. Whatever it was, it had seized his whole attention, freezing him to the spot. As Jonah watched, Sartish came back to himself. He shifted on his feet, shook his head, as if waking, and looked around. Jonah ducked down, hoping that Sartish would not be able to make him out through the glass-stone.

Sartish spoke, his voice strained, thick-sounding. "What do you want of me?"

Jonah eased himself up until he could see over the wall.

"Since when are the Djinn needing human beings?" Sartish said.

Jonah started. *Why is he talking to a Djinn?*

Sartish shook his head. "I know enough. I was in the Tree!" He paused to listen. "You are deceivers. You are seeking to destroy the human race." He listened again. "You call that Tree, that torture, a *fair price?*"

Jonah could just imagine the Djinn's voice—so earnest, reasonable, and logical, so eloquent in the moment . . . He resisted the urge to shout at Sartish. His fists clenched. The sound of blood rushed in his ears.

Sartish shook his head again, as if trying to clear his mind. He spoke, but Jonah could not catch the words. The Djinn must have replied at length. Sartish listened, looking down at his feet. Finally, he said, "I need to think." He paused for the answer, then swatted at the air by his ear. "I need to think! Leave me for now!"

As Sartish hurried back toward the guest quarters, Jonah made his way inside and back to his bed. Sartish came in a few moments later and went straight to his own room. Silence fell, but Jonah knew he would not sleep now. And perhaps, he thought, he would never sleep again. Not after this. After what felt like hours, when he could no longer endure the hurricane in his mind, he rose again and went the balcony.

He was just in time to see the sky turning rose and gold in the east. A few minutes later, the sun pierced the horizon.

* * *

Someone was moving about inside. Jonah looked around. Sartish pushed aside the curtain and stepped onto the balcony.

They regarded each other.

He looks tired, Jonah thought. *I wonder if he slept . . .?*

"They'll come for us soon," he said.

Sartish nodded, his eyes shifting away from Jonah's. He leaned against the balcony wall with both arms folded.

At last, he spoke, his voice softer than Jonah had ever heard it. "I have never witnessed anything like this before."

Jonah nodded. "Yes. They made all this out of sand and light and water."

"So, why not say yes to them?" A fly buzzed around their heads. Sartish swatted at it with more anger than he needed to. Jonah's heart beat a little faster. The Djinn was watching them even now . . .

"Because they don't respect our way," he said. "They don't listen to the Wind."

"*The Wind blows in everything,*" Sartish quoted. "You are always telling me that. That is why you sought their assistance."

He had to bring that up, Jonah thought. *He's been listening after all.* "Yes, I know . . ." he said. "I had hoped that they would reunite with us, as it was in the beginning. But they want us to see their way, or nothing . . ."

"Perhaps we should," Sartish said. "Their way made this.

Where did our way get us? Prisoners on our own island!"

"I can't." Jonah shook his head. "I can't walk away from my own life."

"So, you will say no then," Sartish said, scorn drenching every word. "And we will remain exactly as we were."

Jonah said nothing for a long moment, before shaking his head. "I can't do that either."

"So?" Sartish cried. "What then?"

Again, Jonah paused before replying. "Do you remember when we were in the Blind Watchman's cave together?"

Sartish frowned. "Of course."

"And I told you about Sungula and how he outwitted the Fox and escaped the trap?"

Sartish gestured impatiently. "So?"

"The Wind carried that into my mind at just the right moment. Perhaps It will do the same now, just when we need It."

"Perhaps!" Sartish closed his eyes and ran his fingers through his hair. "Again with this?"

"Listen, Sartish," Jonah said. "You don't have to believe that the Wind will speak. You just have to trust me. Do you?"

Naked anguish filled Sartish's eyes.

"I don't know," he said.

* * *

The audience chamber was crowded when they entered, accompanied by the steward. Jonah guessed that the assembled nobles were the council before which he was expected to kneel. They parted before the steward, who carried a staff and looked as if he would happily wield it to clear the way. The last of the nobles stepped aside, revealing the island platform where the

Mighty One sat, the Prime Minister at his shoulder as before. The steward bowed low and, without a word, marched back where he came from.

Tasarakt leaned forward. "Where is your third companion, the lost son of Mezoramia?"

"He . . ." Jonah said. "He did not return to the guest quarters last night, Mighty One."

Tasarakt glanced over his shoulder at the Prime Minister, and they shared a smile.

"Of course not," Tasarakt said. "He has come home. Now, what is your answer, foreigner?"

Jonah stared at him. All the way down through the maze of corridors and stairways, across the courtyard and up the steps to the Mighty One's house, he had searched inside himself for the words, any words. But nothing came. A kind of blank despair—doldrums in which the breath of the Wind had died away, leaving utter silence—had absorbed every thought inside of him, leaving him paralyzed, speechless.

"Well?" Tasarakt said, frowning. "Speak!"

"You are wasting the Mighty One's time!" the Prime Minister added.

Jonah could feel Sartish's eyes burning on the side of his face, but for some reason, he could not turn to look at him.

"Just say yes," Sartish whispered fiercely. "The People need us!"

Jonah opened his mouth, but the blankness enveloped his tongue.

"I . . ." he finally managed.

"What?" Tasarakt said. "Answer at once!"

"How can you ask a man to leave the place where his heart rests?" Bas Rabyah said. Sartish and Jonah spun around. Every head in the room had turned, the silence breaking into a scandalized hubbub. Bas Rabyah stood at the entrance of the audience chamber, leaning on a staff. He wore traditional Mezoramian white robes, which bestowed on the old man a strange new dignity that Jonah had not seen before now.

Bas Rabyah strode forward, the nobles parting before him. Closer up, Jonah noticed the exhaustion etched under his eyes.

The Prime Minister's hands fluttered like agitated birds. "What is the meaning of this outrageous interruption?"

Tasarakt leaned forward. "What is your business with foreigners, Son of Bastamy?"

Bas Rabyah strolled forward, and bowed low. "An excellent question, Mighty One. A question I have been pondering for three days. At first, my mind was clouded as the memories came back to me, and suddenly, I no longer felt like a stranger. You cannot imagine . . ." he closed his eyes at the joy of it. "I wandered through the marketplaces. I tasted honey-soaked dates for the first time in a lifetime! They were my favorite as a child. And the wine! A little too much of that, I admit. But still, it took me back . . ."

"So, why are you here?" Tasarakt said. "Return to your ancestral home. If there is any dispute, I will support your claim . . ."

Bas Rabyah raised one hand. "Please. Forgive me." The Prime Minister looked horrified at the interruption, but Bas ignored him. "It was indeed pleasant to visit my former life. But there is a reason that the past is past. Resurrected memories are sweet, but I cannot relive them as they were. I have seen too much. I cannot go back to believing that the world is smaller than it really is. I am truly dead to this life."

Bas Rabyah turned to Jonah. "If you choose to kneel, I will

kneel too. Not as a son returning to his father, but as a foreigner making an alliance on behalf his People and the home of his heart. If, however, you choose not to kneel, I will follow you into the desert, wherever you go, until death comes for me a second time."

Something surged up in Jonah. "You don't have to do this, Bas." His words caught in his throat. "You owe us nothing . . ."

Bas Rabyah smiled, his eyes bright. "You are a worthy successor to the Elder. I owed him a debt, but to you I give freely."

The confidence that had deserted Jonah swept back in full force, the Wind in the form of a hurricane. Whatever followed from this moment, he was certain of one thing—he would not be alone. He glanced at Sartish, saw the dismay spreading over his face, as if he knew what was going to happen next . . .

At least he knows me that well, Jonah thought. He stepped forward and raised his chin. "Thank you for your offer, Mighty One. Respectfully, my companions and I must decline to kneel. We will find another way."

Tasarakt's mouth set in a grim line. He leaned back. "As you wish, fool. I am done with you. As for you," he said to Bas Rabyah. "You should be ashamed. You were given a second life and you used it to dishonor your people and commit apostasy from the way of the pure Light." He turned the Prime Minister. "Have them escorted to the main gate. Let them walk back to their island, if they can!"

The Prime Minister smiled with a touch of relish and called out, "Guards!"

The soldiers stepped forward. Jonah and Bas Rabyah turned away to follow them, but Sartish stood his ground.

"No," he said.

Jonah closed his eyes. Somehow, anticipating this moment had not prepared him for the blunt force of it in his heart. A voice spoke in his mind. *Sometimes the Wind must blow us away before It can blow us back . . .*

"I will kneel," Sartish said. He pointed at Jonah. "He would entrust us to nothing more than a breath, but we need flesh and blood! We need someone with armies and weapons, or we will certainly perish at the hands of the Djinn's servants. For all our People, I am kneeling and asking Mezoramia to be our protector!"

Tasarakt looked back and forth between Jonah and Sartish, nonplussed.

"What do you say to this?" he asked Jonah at last.

"Nothing," Jonah said, meeting Sartish's eyes. "Anyone who chooses to follow him can do so. If the Wind so chooses it."

"Chooses?" Tasarakt demanded. "How does it choose?"

Jonah shrugged. "There is a way."

"What way?" Tasarakt demanded.

"We call it the Ordeal of Windfire," Jonah said.

Sartish shifted. Tasarakt saw his discomfort, and frowned. "Describe this ordeal."

"Anyone who takes the Lamp must be tested by Windfire," Jonah said.

"And if they fail this test?" Tasarakt persisted.

Jonah shrugged again. "They are destroyed."

The Mighty One leaned back. "You mean," he said slowly, "no one can hold this Lamp unless it finds him worthy?"

"Not exactly," Jonah said.

Tasarakt waved impatiently. "Essentially, this is the matter. And you have undergone this ordeal. Correct?"

Jonah inclined his head. "Yes. When the Elder gave me—"

"And you have not?" Tasarakt said to Sartish.

"I will take it—" Sartish said.

"But you have not yet," Tasarakt said. "And we do not know if you will survive."

Sartish was silent, jaw clenched. Tasarakt gestured at the Prime Minister. As they held a low conversation, Jonah watched him, heart pounding. His thoughts whirled at the sudden unexpected turn of events. Until Sartish had spoken, he had resigned himself to death in the desert. Now . . .

Tasarakt nodded and waved the Prime Minister away. He turned back to them, tugging at his robe to straighten it.

"Given this new revelation," he said, his voice raised to carry to every corner of the audience chamber. "I rescind my order to expel the foreigners from the Floating City." In the uproar that followed, the Prime Minister thumped his staff. Once there was silence, the Mighty One continued. "Instead, they will accompany us back to their homeland, this one as our latest vassal," he indicated Sartish, "and his former companion as our prisoner. When our army has put the servants of the Djinn to flight, the foreigners can decide among themselves who will govern them on our behalf. Or we will choose for them. In either case, they and their power will serve Mezoramia, to the glory of the Light!"

A cheer rose up, and a round of applause.

"As for the former son and apostate Bas Rabyah," Tasarakt added. "I have no need of him. Cast him out of the City!"

The guards closed around Bas Rabyah, the old man's face grieving but stoic.

"Wait!" Jonah cried. "Let him come with us. I will cooper-ate!"

"No, Lord Elder," Bas Rabyah said. "Not for my sake!"

Tasarakt's eyebrows rose. "You will kneel?" he said to Jonah.

"I cannot follow your way," Jonah said. "But I will obey your just laws, and I will urge my People to do the same."

Silence had fallen over the audience chamber. Tasarakt looked around, seeing the eyes of his courtiers fixed on him.

"Very well," he said at last. He raised his voice over the noise. "But if you attempt to escape or incite rebellion, your friend's life will be forfeit. He will *beg* for exile when I am finished with him. Do you understand?"

"I understand," Jonah said.

Disagree

As steward's mate, Disagree threw himself into his work with such dedication that the angry little man whose club foot prevented him from joining the others in raids could find no excuse to use his cane for anything other than walking. As a sign of his pleasure, the steward did not force Disagree to serve the tables and endure the taunts of the crew but sent him to scrub pots instead. Disagree obeyed with obsessive intensity, trying to erase with his hands the memory of the Captain turning away . . .

He made his way to his hammock in the common area long after everyone else was asleep. He lay awake, replaying everything over and over, as if it would produce a different outcome. At last, exhaustion overtook him. The grief swept back full force, and he no longer had the strength to fight the tears, pressing his pillow against his face to muffle the sound. Only then did sleep take hold of him at last.

Before dawn, he stumbled into the galley, where the steward was preparing the Captain's breakfast. Another crewmember came to collect the tray, throwing a spiteful glance at Disagree as she hurried away. In that moment, the grief of the previous night flipped into a sudden resentment for the Captain.

Just because a boy gets sick when he sees a man tortured, for this he turns his back?

Galvanized, he went at his assigned tasks with an energy that could be mistaken for vengeance. Between the slop work of the pots and scrubbing the floors, he convinced the steward to let him help with the cooking. A few evenings later, the steward allowed him to make the fish stew for the Captain's supper. When the Captain sent compliments, a wave of triumph had swept over Disagree, only to recede a moment later. *He* should have been waiting at the Captain's table, ladling the stew into his bowl . . .

One morning, the lookout sighted the Claw-men's last hunting ground. When the call came down from the crow's nest, even the steward abandoned the galley. Disagree hung back. He had avoided the Captain all this time, and the thought of an encounter both tore at him and compelled him. At last, he followed the others, his feet dragging him down with each step he took up the ladder.

The hunting ground was a large body of water inside a circle of low-lying islands covered with scrub and inhabited by crabs, nesting cormorants, and tortoises. To Disagree, they resembled beads of a necklace on the water.

Hanging back to keep out of sight, he watched the fleet approach the edge of the atoll and drop anchor. At once, the other ships lowered skiffs to the water and raced each other through the breakers. The rowers hauled to gain an advantage over the others as gunners crouched amidships, rifles ready. On *La Justice*, the first mate was about to follow suit. Captain Hodoul belayed the order. Bewildered, the crew watched, grumbling as the other hunting parties scoured the lagoons for dragons.

At sunset, Disagree came up to watch boats return to their ships, empty-handed. On *La Justice*, the Captain ordered an extra share of rum with their rations, as a consolation for not joining the hunt. Disagree returned to the galley to open kegs and fill mugs to the brim, but the work seemed little more than drudgery now, drowned in the anticipation. What would the Captain do the next day?

The following morning, the other crews sent their boats out again, and again Hodoul forbade his men from joining them. Concealed under the overhang of the poop deck, Disagree heard the first mate asking in a trembling voice why they were delaying—wouldn't they forfeit their share of the prizes? The Captain's answer was cold. "With those fools beating the water to a froth out there, of course they aren't catching anything. We'll let them exhaust themselves and clear the field a little before we act."

By the end of the third day, most of the ships had given up and weighed anchor for home. They must have decided to make do with whatever Claw they had raided from the storehouses. Other than *La Justice*, only the four largest ships remained: a three-mast dhow, a schooner, a man-o'-war, and a junk. Disagree knew the captains of those crews. They had attended many of Hodoul's night-time audiences and were his most intractable and cunning opponents, the biggest obstacle in his effort to unite the Brethren under his Overlord-given authority. If the Captain had a plan, they would be there to foil it.

Just after sunset, Disagree was absently stacking the pots and bowls, his mind lost in speculations about what the Captain's strategy might be—when the first mate shouted from above, his exultant voice cutting through the din of the galley. "Strongest arms to launch and man the skiffs. At once!"

The crew abandoned their bowls of fish stew and shoved and jostled their way out the door, clearing the mess in seconds. The

Steward muttered something about wasted food, but he could not resist the temptation to hobble after them, Disagree close behind him. The main deck was dark—the moon had not risen yet. Around him the crew crowded close, watching in silence as several of the best rowers lowered three skiffs over the port side. The Captain himself was overseeing them, striding back and forth, reminding them in a metallic undertone to slow down, so the sheaves wouldn't squeal.

Disagree smiled to himself. The Captain must have ordered them to hold their tongues on pain of a hanging. The other crews would see that they were launching soon enough. They needed the element of surprise.

The skiffs touched the surface with a faint *splash*. The crews clambered down and set oars—wrapped in dampers—to the oarlocks. The Captain turned to the first mate. "Do you have it?" The first mate handed over something with a faint *clink*. The Captain pocketed the object, then clambered down out of sight. As the skiffs drew away from *La Justice* and drove in through the reef, the Captain stood in the bow of the lead boat, balancing against the hull's movements with both hands in his pockets.

A passionate longing surged up in Disagree, making it difficult to breathe. He wanted more than anything to be the one rowing that skiff into whatever danger lay ahead. He no longer cared if Hodoul, the only father he had ever known, never looked at him again. He didn't care if another boy or girl came to live upstairs in the mansion as the Captain's chosen heir. Disagree would happily live in the servant's quarters for the rest of his life—cooking or cleaning, serving or waiting to serve, walking behind the Captain, or rowing, or even carrying him wherever he needed to go and whenever he asked.

Disagree pushed his way through the crew until he reached the railing, leaning forward to get a clear view. The skiff had just passed through the line of the reef, surfing the breakers. The moon had broken over the horizon, spilling light over the ocean. A cry went up from one of the nearby ships—the hunting party had been spotted. Almost at once, the other ships took up the alarm. Torches flared on the decks as the crews scrambled to launch their own boats in pursuit of Hodoul's party. They had been watching, Disagree realized, just waiting for him to do something like this. They knew him well.

Safely inside the lagoon, Captain Hodoul's rowers pulled on. Even from here, Disagree sensed the Captain's calm, as if the imminent challenge of his rivals meant nothing to him. Skiffs fanned out on either side, the lead boat at the center. There was a faint *thunk* of oars drawn in and stowed away. Men moved back and forth, and then fell into the stillness of waiting. Hodoul was a statue, clearly visible, his angular form outlined in the moonlight, his hair glowing. Disagree could not make out the barrels of rifles silhouetted against the glittering expanse of water. How would they kill the dragon?

On the other ships, the skiffs dropped to the waters, their pulleys squealing. Their crews drove into the reef, tossing and bouncing through the surf as the rowers hauled. The custom was clear and indisputable, even by Brethren standards. If Hodoul killed the dragon, the prize was his alone. If the rival hunting parties managed to get a rope around it before that happened, they could claim their own share.

Hodoul raised his arm. High above the surf, a bell chimed—a single chime, a double, a single chime again. Disagree recognized that sound. It was the little hand-bell that the Captain used to summon him to his cabin. That must have been what the first mate gave him. But why would he need to ring . . .?

A thought flashed into his mind. *Maybe he calls . . .* But even before he could articulate the words, the water inside the half-circle of boats boiled and exploded, and a dragon—all sharp edges and barnacles and draped with seaweed—rose above the surface, beating its stubby wings and kicking up spray.

Despite the risk of losing their claim on the prize, the approaching rival hunters broke off their frenetic rowing. The Captain's crew also froze as the monster loomed above them. Then it shrieked, arched back, like a snake about to descend into its strike, and Captain Hodoul bellowed, "Hooks! Now, you fools!"

His voice brought them back. There was an urgent movement among the men. The dark shapes of grappling hooks soared toward the dragon. As they landed, the dragon shrieked again and jerked back. Several yards away, the rival parties were racing at them again, hoping to get their own grappling hooks into the monster before Hodoul's crew opened fire. And in the midst of this, the Captain stood his ground in the bow of his boat, oblivious to the commotion around him, his head flung back.

Disagree gripped the railing. On the rival boats, the hunters were on their feet, hefting grappling hooks as the rowers continued to haul, foam creaming at the bows and along the sides. As soon as they were in range, they would launch their hooks, and whatever happened after that, they would be fighting it out with Hodoul's crew over the prize. The fragile accord for which the Captain had worked would be over.

"Shoot it!" Disagree muttered.

The man beside him looked sideways. "They didn't take rifles."

Disagree looked at him and frowned. "What? Why?"

The man shrugged. "I didn't ask. I like my skin too much."

Disagree didn't have time to consider this new information, because something was happening with the dragon. Its frantic bucking and tossing had suddenly yielded to a gentle swaying motion, as if it had heard something it recognized, the strains of some primordial lullaby. Its head sagged and sank lower with each sway, the beating of its wings slackening, until it collapsed onto the surface in another explosion of spray and waves, nearly capsizing the boats. As the monster's body hit, Hodoul, burst into movement. He leaped from the bow onto the dragon's body, scrambled up as high onto its spine as he could, using the scales as handholds, then straightened and raised a fist.

"This prize is mine!" he shouted to the approaching crews. "The prize is mine!"

* * *

It was nearly midnight when the boats finally managed to haul the dragon's massive sleeping body—its nostrils blowing steam like the blowhole of a whale—through a nearby gap in the reef, and back to *La Justice*.

Under the first mate's direction, as the Captain shouted instructions from his position on the dragon's back, the rest of the crew, Disagree among them, hauled a spare anchor chain from the bowels of the ship, secured one end to the bollards, and lowered the other over the aft rail. After the boats had maneuvered the dragon into the lee of the stern, the Captain personally locked the chain around its neck with several padlocks, before returning to the ship. The prize was now his, beyond dispute.

The rival boats hovered nearby until the dragon was secured and truly beyond their reach. They retreated to their ships, only to return within minutes, this time manned by only two crewmen and carrying one passenger. Even from a distance, Disagree knew that the rival captains were on the way.

They came on deck, one after the other, standing opposite Captain Hodoul, who watched them with cool amusement. Close on either side and high above in the rigging, his crewmen leaned forward to catch every word. The conversation that followed would provide months of gossip to fill their idle moments.

Of all the captains, Disagree knew that the one to watch was Madame Razor. She was a tall Amazonian figure, her hair pleated in ornate patterns around her head. From the Captain's hints and comments, Disagree had gathered that Hodoul had known her in some way in the lower world of the Lethes—a mistress, perhaps, or his wife. Among the Brethren, their relationship had devolved in a series of very public quarrels, which all culminated in a knife fight that left the Captain with a near fatal chest wound. Since then, she had expanded her crew into the second largest, after Hodoul's. She had signed the Code, but her crew had violated it more than all the others combined. Now, Disagree could tell from the way the other captains stood behind her that she had them under her control too.

"How may I help you, fellow Brethren?" Hodoul said.

"You know very well, my dear Jack," Madame Razor replied, hands on hips. "We contest your claim to the prize!"

"For what reason?" Hodoul asked, in a mild tone.

"You had an unfair advantage," one of the captains, Torteau, croaked.

"What you call unfair advantage, I call simple foresight," Hodoul replied. "While your crews were killing every Claw-man and stealing every bag of Claw in sight, I was thinking ahead to when the supply runs out. What are we going to do when that happens, eh? Did you stop to think about that?"

They said nothing.

"Well, *I* did," Hodoul said. "I concerned myself with the one person who could extend the supply indefinitely."

"Even so," Madame Razor said at last. "You should have shared what you learned from the Claw-man with us!"

Hodoul shook his head, as if she were a recalcitrant child. "So we could fight it out trying to decide how to cut that beast into five equal pieces? Even if that worked, we would eventually be right back where we started. We'd spend the rest of our days hunting for more dragons, and who knows how many are left?"

He allowed this information to sink in, amused to see the dismay spreading in the faces of the other Captains and the crew, who now contemplated the rest of their lives without an acrid breath of Claw to relieve them.

"So," Madame Razor said. "What, then?"

Hodoul inclined his head. "My proposal is simple. You name me as your king, and I will appoint the four of you my princes. We will sign treaties of alliance, one to each other, and there will be peace. I will use my knowledge to harvest Claw from the dragon regularly. You and I can negotiate to ensure that every member of every crew has regular access to a supply of what he or she needs to get by."

In the silence and darkness overhead, the wind hummed in the rigging.

"But you would control the supply," Madame Razor said at last, in a flat voice.

"Isn't that what a king does?" Hodoul said. "Give life to his people?" He grinned—an almost shocking expression for him.

Madame Razor did not return the smile. "Fine." She ignored the discomfort of the other captains. "Draw up the treaties."

As the crew broke into excited chatter, Hodoul smiled and clapped his hands. "Excellent! Shall we drink to our alliance?"

Madame Razor smiled for the first time, and Disagree understood again why her crew were willing to die for her.

"Captain Le Moray is always prepared for such requests," she said.

Le Moray had already produced a small bottle of rum. "From my finest batch," he cried. "For only the best occasions!"

"And I can't think of a better occasion than this one," Hodoul replied. "Steward!"

The steward took the bottle from Le Moray and hurried below, Disagree following close behind. In the galley, the steward cracked the seal off the bottle and filled five crystal goblets on a silver tray. "Take it up," he told Disagree. "And for every drop you spill, I will spill a drop of your blood with my cane!"

Disagree took the stairs one a time, watching the ripples on the surface of each goblet. On deck, he went around offering the tray first to each of the captains, and then to Hodoul. As the Captain glanced at him for the first time, Disagree's hands trembled. He took a deep breath, lowered his eyes and stepped back.

Madame Razor raised her goblet. "To a new era of peace and prosperity!"

She glanced sideways at the other captains, who also raised their goblets, echoing her sentiment in a ragged chorus.

"Peace and prosperity!"

Hodoul raised his goblet, watching them. The pause drew

out.

He's waiting for them to drink first, Disagree thought. *In case . .*
.

Madame Razor smiled, as if she understood. "A long life, my dear Jack." She raised the goblet to her lips and drank. The other captains did the same, but there was a touch of hesitation about it, and one of them, Torteau, coughed before he obeyed. Disagree knew that cough—it was one of the signs of his anxiety.

But why? he thought. *If it's not poisoned . . .*

For some reason, the Captain hadn't noticed the cough. Perhaps he was distracted, riding the wave of victory . . . Either way, he appeared satisfied at seeing his rivals take the first drink, and brought his goblet to his lips.

Disagree snatched the goblet. "I taste it first," he said, and drank.

As the liquor ran down his throat like liquid fire, all the captains gaped at him.

"How dare you?" Hodoul said. "Who the hell do you think—?" Then he glanced at the captains, saw the horror on their faces, and understanding dawned at last. But it was too late. His features swam in front of Disagree's eyes. The brilliance of the morning light dimmed and turned grey, as if the sun had decided to set again. Then all the light, the faces around him, were sucked into a roaring tornado of darkness.

Disagree's legs gave way. He collapsed face first on the deck.

* * *

The roaring receded. The dark unconsciousness yielded to something more palpable. Then he opened his eyes. He knew where he was right away—in the Captain's cabin, in his bed.

Through the aft windows, the moon threw glittering reflections on the expanse of the ocean. The other ships had disappeared from view.

They must have set sail, he thought. The short-lived alliance was over.

The door creaked, and Captain Hodoul ducked in, holding up an oil lamp. He approached the bed, saw that Disagree was awake, and nodded, the relief appearing on his face—and vanishing as almost at once.

He laid the lamp on the bedside table, sat down at the edge of the bed, and regarded Disagree with his customary calm.

"So, it seems they didn't want to parlay after all," he said. "All they wanted was to remove me, one way or another."

"What happen to them?" Disagree said.

"I allowed them to leave the ship alive," Hodoul said, "on the condition that they provide the antidote. They will be back, when they run out of Claw and get desperate. And then they will submit to me, like it or not."

Disagree said nothing. As usual, no answer was necessary.

"I should have seen it," Hodoul went on. "But I was too caught up, thinking that we were getting somewhere at last . . ." He stared away into the distance, speaking more to himself that to Disagree. "I lost focus. I didn't read the signs. I didn't even guess that they might have taken the antidote ahead of time . . ."

He turned his eyes back to Disagree. "How did you know?"

Disagree shook his head. "I do not know," he croaked, his throat burned with each word. "I just know you are in danger."

Hodoul nodded. "Well, it was enough. I saved your life once, and now you have saved mine. Your debt is paid." He stared down at the bed without seeing it. "I still believe that you could not follow my path. But, after this, I can offer you one thing." He leaned forward and gripped Disagree's arm. "You can be my right arm for as long as I live. I know it is not everything you were hoping for . . ."

Disagree met his eyes. The joy rose up like a clear fountain inside him.

"It is all I ever want," he said.

II

Part Two

Chapter Six

Isabella soared upwards in a river of light, which swirled and eddied over her skin. Both near to her and further in the distance, she could distinguish other streams like hers, reverse tributaries flowing to an ocean in the sky.

The liquid light now thickened, turning oily and sluggish. Her rapid ascent slowed, and finally stopped. She had come to ground. The light drained away, as if into some kind of swamp. Darkness engulfed her again, a solid darkness in which she was buried, encased. Sand poured into her mouth and nose.

Isabella choked, coughed, and held her breath. She scrabbled around, trying to dig her way upward, but the particles were too quick and fine and offered her hands and feet no purchase. She felt her lungs spasm and catch fire and opened her mouth to take the breath that would suffocate her. A hand—thin, small, and unusually strong—pushed down from above, grabbed her wrist, and hauled her out.

Isabella lay now on what felt like grass, coughing and blinded, but breathing.

The voice of a young girl spoke. "You are unburied, mademoiselle."

Isabella sat up, coughing, rubbed her eyes, and peered. The girl came slowly into focus. She was no more than six or seven years old, with olive skin, a sweet round face, and kinky hair woven into plaits.

"I'm Shantih," the girl said, smiling. "Welcome to Mysterion."

Isabella tried to reply, but a fit of coughing seized her. Finally, she managed to croak out her name. "Isabella . . ."

Shantih reached out her hand. "I know. I'm so glad you came back to us."

Isabella took Shantih's hand, frowning. Then she remembered. "You were with Jonah. You brought us *tec-tec* soup."

"Yes," Shantih nodded. "I take care of him, like the Elder before him." A faint longing touched her voice. "Where is he?"

"I left him at the Falls," Isabella said. Another memory returned to her: Jonah raising his hand in farewell as Sartish pulled the skiff slowly away from the ship, enveloped in the mist and thunder of the nearby Falls.

"He must have entered Sleep," Shantih said. "To come and find you among the Lethes."

"Yes. He was there. He taught me to kindle the Lamp. It took a while. I'm a slow learner." She smiled crookedly.

Shantih reached out and stroked her cheek. "Don't worry, Bella-Bella. Everyone takes their own time to find their way to Mysterion. But not the Elder. He only ever takes one night. When it's bedtime, he enters into Sleep. He may live in the dream of the Lethes for days or months or years, but even if it takes all that time for them to learn the Lamp, his work is always finished when the sun comes up."

"So he may be on his way back?" Isabella said. There was something about the little girl that was both young and very old.

"Yes." Shantih's face clouded. "But it's been almost two months. With Azrel's help, he should be back already."

Isabella considered this. Then something occurred to her. "Are the Brethren still here?"

Shantih face grew darker still. "Yes. They keep on trying to get up the mountain, but the Lamp won't let them. Then they get angry and shout bad things at us. And we hear them at night, singing and fighting."

Another of Isabella's memories surfaced: a pirate—Guillotine—disappearing in flash of brilliance from the Lamp.

"Maybe Jonah went to get some help to break the siege," she suggested.

The light returned to Shantih's face. "Really? You think so?"

Isabella wasn't sure, but she nodded. "The Wind will blow him back, when It's ready."

Shantih nodded quickly. "Yes. Of course it will!" Excitement took hold of her. "Come. Let's go and meet the People!"

Dragging Isabella to her feet, she led her at a run through the forest. The trees were tall and well-spaced, with little in the way of undergrowth. Instead the ground was covered, as far as Isabella could see, with pools. As they passed, Isabella caught glimpses of visions reflected in the surface of each of them:

The fish market on a busy day, women in colorful dresses and hats haggling with fishermen over their morning catch;

A procession of girls in white dresses, holding bouquets as they made their way up to a church for their First Communion.

Then there were other strange images from places that Isabella did not recognize:

A snowy mountaintop fortress at night, where guards patrolled the ramparts by the light of flaming torches;

The peaks of pyramids in the jungle, where white-robed priests raised golden staffs, chanting toward the sky;

A city made of some glass-like stone, surrounded by the

endless desert dunes.

Isabella wanted to pause and examine these uncountable, fascinating sights, but Shantih would not slow her pace.

"You bring us hope, Bella-Bella," she panted. "Your presence here is hopeful."

"Why me?" Isabella panted. Her muscles trembled and ached at each step, as if her legs were unaccustomed to use.

"Every day I go and see the pools of the Lethes," Shantih said. "As many as the forest lets me. When I see one of them that is dried up, I know that someone is ready to come out. But all this time, there were no dry pools, and the People were getting sad. They thought the pirate king had killed the Elder . . . Now they'll know he's still alive, because of you, Bella-Bella. Oh, here we are!" She exclaimed, pointing ahead, where the trees thinned. "Sometimes it takes hours for the forest to let me leave."

They emerged from the forest onto a broad plateau dotted with lean-tos. A hundred or so yards ahead, the land ended at a cliff, and beyond, the ocean stretched away, ruffled green and white-capped in the wind.

Nearby, groups of people seated on the grass turned to stare at them. From the lean-tos, curious heads looked out.

"Come and see!" She called out to them. "Isabella is unburied!"

The People of the Wind hurried over, gathering around her and Isabella. Their faces, lined and strained, relaxed and brightened somewhat at the news that the Elder was alive, and had woken one of the Lethes.

The first to embrace her was an old man with skin like dusty charcoal and silver threads of hair, neatly parted.

"I remember you!" he exclaimed. "It didn't take you long at

all. I already had a foot in the grave when *I* was unburied!"

"I'm sorry . . ." Isabella said, frowning, a little taken aback at the old man's familiarity.

"They call me Regent," the old man said. "But I am always just old Pierre."

"Oh yes!" Isabella recalled Jonah handing Pierre the Lamp, the old man bowing his white head. She returned his embrace.

"Isabella, where is the Elder?" a woman called out of the crowd.

Others called out questions: "When will he return?" "Why is he taking so long?"

Pierre turned and raised his hands. "Beloved ones, he will return!" he said. "Isabella is proof that he has not left us."

"How do we know?" a male voice, more aggressive and angrier than the rest, called out. "Why should we believe it?"

The crowd fell silent. Isabella could feel their anxiety returning, the tension rising. The speaker—a thin, pale, sullen-looking man—pushed his way forward through the crowd and confronted them, arms folded.

"When will he be back?" he demanded.

"I don't know," Isabella admitted.

The People looked at one another. The man took courage from their unhappiness and drew himself upright.

"Then how do we know he's not out there somewhere, with not a mind to come back? Maybe we're on our own!"

"We know because we have faith, Dio," Pierre said. "As we always do."

"And what about taking responsibility, eh?" Dio cried. "Are we going to be doing any of that any time soon?"

"The Elder has given us a responsibility—"

"To do what?" Dio cried. "Sit on our backsides on the top of a mountain like sheep?"

"When you reach a certain vintage," Pierre said, "you will learn that staying still is sometimes the best you can do."

"Don't patronize me, old man!" Dio shouted. The crowd gasped in shock. Shantih was staring at Dio with wide eyes.

"These are just soft little excuses," Dio said. "The Elder's gone off to someplace peaceful, maybe in the east with the Solitaries. If he's still working to bring back the Lethes, that's where he is. And now it's up to us to get ourselves down off this mountain and away from those pirates! As a matter of fact," he raised his voice as the crowd murmured amongst themselves, "why do we have to run away like frightened children? We have the most powerful weapon in the world on our side!" Dio flung out his hand. Following his gesture, Isabella noticed a carved lamp-post planted at the edge of the plateau. Hanging from it was the Lamp she had kindled in the cemetery.

Isabella recalled what Jonah had said, that the Lamp existed both here and among the Lethes. She hadn't understood it at the time. She still didn't, yet, somehow it made sense. In the world she had known—even now receding into the shadows of her memory—the Lamp was the only bright thing, a piece of Mysterion in a world of forgetfulness. The Lamp had guided her here. She had simply cooperated.

"We can carry the Lamp in front of us down the mountain," Dio was saying, "and finish those pirates once and for all. If any of them survive and get away, they won't be creeping back here any time soon!"

"The Lamp was never intended for that purpose!" Pierre trembled with rage. "It was given to protect, not kill!"

"Protection!" Dio scoffed. "How did the old Elder use the Lamp the first time? He burned up the Djinn! Why not us?"

Pierre's anger came upon Isabella. She rounded on Dio. "I saw the Elder today, and I know he's coming back!"

"And who are you?" Dio sneered. "The last time we saw *you*, you had come to kill the Elder! Now you have advice?"

Pierre stepped toward Dio, his fists bunched. "All the Unburied have an equal voice," he thundered. "Besides, I am Regent. Everyone saw the Elder give me that responsibility. My decision is final. We remain!"

Dio opened his mouth, but Pierre held up a hand. "Unless," he said, "you would like to take up the Lamp yourself?"

Dio's pale face drained of all color. He closed his mouth. His fists clenched and unclenched. Finally, he turned and shoved his way out of the crowd. Pierre watched him go with a stricken expression.

"I told him, this is not for me," he mumbled. For the first time, he sounded his age.

"Why wouldn't he take the Lamp?" Isabella asked.

Pierre didn't answer, watching the crowd disperse, more subdued than ever.

Shantih spoke in the silence. "The Lamp tests anyone who takes it."

"Windfire," Isabella said, the name of it coming back to her.

Pierre nodded reluctantly. "Yes. It burns away whatever is not of the Wind."

"So he's afraid that the Windfire might destroy him?" Isabella said. "But isn't he one of the People? Isn't he safe?"

"Anyone who takes the Lamp the first time experiences the ordeal of Windfire," Pierre said, as if Isabella were being unfair to Dio. "It is terrifying and painful, even if your whole heart *does* belong to the Wind."

"Perhaps he's afraid that it doesn't . . ." Isabella said.

Pierre swatted the suggestion away. "Dio will do as he will. And we must trust that the Wind will blow him where he needs to go in the end. For now," he went on, "I am certain that little Shantih already has lunch ready. She will take care of you." He smiled down at the little girl. "Life is quiet here, but you will soon find a place. Perhaps you can help Shantih check the Pools every day . . ."

It was obvious to Isabella that the subject was closed. She allowed Shantih to lead her away to get some lunch. In the weeks that followed, Isabella tried to follow Pierre's direction, and put Dio out of her mind. In the mornings, after a simple breakfast of tea and breadfruit boiled in coconut milk, she accompanied Shantih on her rounds through the forest to see if any of the Pools were dry. This at least gave her the opportunity to gaze at the reflections and wonder at some of the visions they contained. She spent the afternoons playing with the children, and after the evening meal, the People gathered to dance—men and women facing each other in lines as they stepped in time to a fiddler's tune.

Although this routine filled much of her time, Isabella still found opportunities to wander along the edge of the plateau. She got used to seeing the pirate sentries at the base of the mountain, dozing away the heat of the day, or playing dice. Sometimes they catcalled or taunted her, but mostly they kept to themselves. She followed the edge of the plateau all the way around, examining each of the more than one hundred Brethren ships that formed the blockade, anchored at even intervals around the island. *La Justice* was not among them. Disagree must still be sailing back from the East with *him*. As the days wore on with no sign of *La Justice*, she gave up on her self-imposed patrol and planted herself on a rock, scanning the horizon until Shantih came to find her.

"There you are, Bella-Bella! Don't worry. The Elder will be back soon, as you said. Come, it's time for supper . . ."

Isabella nodded and smiled and took the little girl's hand, but her heart was troubled. How could she tell Shantih that it wasn't Azrel and Jonah she had been looking for, but the black sails of *La Justice*?

Dio did nothing to ease her guilt. After their confrontation, he had decided that he wasn't going to let things go and had started a campaign to win support for his cause among the People. Every day, Isabella caught sight of him in the midst of a group of three or four people, talking in a low voice, jabbing in the air with one hand to make his points while those around him regarded him with perplexed, conflicted expressions. She knew that the longer they had to wait, the more compelling his arguments would become. And if they decided that Jonah wasn't going to return after all, that he had stayed among the Solitaries, then leaving the plateau might seem the only way out . . .

She brought her fears to Pierre and found herself blocked by the old man's sanguine take on the situation. Whatever she said, whatever argument she put forward, he always repeated variations on the same theme. "The Wind will blow Dio where he needs to go."

Isabella closed her eyes. "And if he's not following the Wind? You're willing to risk him leading the People into death . . ."

"We are not there yet!" Pierre snapped. "You are young here. Leave Dio to his course, and mind yourself for now."

"You're ignoring the facts," Isabella flared. "It's obvious that he's planning—" Shrieks interrupted her. A crowd of children raced through the camp, calling in chorus, "A pirate ship! A pirate ship is coming!"

Isabella and Pierre raced for the edge of the plateau, while Shantih and others trailed behind. At the edge of the cliff, the crowd swelled until the entire population watched in silence as *La Justice* ran down toward the island, her black sails spread like wings, her metal hull reflecting the morning sunlight.

Pierre spoke first, his voice soft with dismay. "He is back. Hodoul is back."

Shantih took Isabella's hand. Isabella looked down at the distress in the little girl's face, and guilt assailed her. Seeing the gleaming black ship, her own feelings had surged in opposite directions—hatred that Hodoul's name sparked in her and surging joy at the prospect of seeing Dis's face once again.

Chapter Seven

A bluebottle fly winged its way over a storm-tossed ocean. Black clouds rushed overhead, driven east, first exposing and then concealing the full moon, which threw a flat brilliant light over the scene. The waves, obsidian black and crested with white foam, marched in rows before the face of the wind. The bluebottle sped onward with a strange single-mindedness, unnatural for its kind. Even the combined buffeting of wind and water could not throw it off the arrow-straight line of its path.

The clouds again unclothed the moon, revealing *La Justice* a few leagues ahead. Her hull gleamed like oiled cast iron. She heeled over under full sail, her leeward railing digging into the turbulent waters.

The fly reached the ship, buzzed over the poop deck, where a sleepy crewman kept watch by the light of a lantern, then down below deck, crawling under the door into the king's quarters. It circled the Master's four poster bed, then alighted on the pillow beside the head of the man it had travelled several days to confront. King Hodoul lay with hands folded on his chest, and the peaceful empty expression so common in the dead. But as soon as the bluebottle touched the pillow, his eyes snapped open.

"I am surprised it took you so long to get to me, Malach," he said.

The response, spoken in rich deep tones, emanated not from the fly at all, but spoke directly into the king's mind.

I thought I'd give you a chance to reflect on the foolishness of your choices.

"If I am being called a fool," Hodoul said, "I would like to see my accuser face to face."

He rose with abrupt energy, tossing his covers aside. The insect rose into the air and traced circles overhead as Hodoul brought a lamp over to the table. A warm glow diffused itself through the cabin. Hodoul went to the washstand and brought a basin, sloshing, into the full light of the lantern. As he leaned over the troubled water, the fly hovered by his head. A muscular Djinn with a head like an ox's skull, spreading horns, and pterodactyl-like wings grinned up at Hodoul from the water.

Better? Malach's mouth moved, but his voice continued to speak into Hodoul's mind.

"Much," Hodoul said. "Now, you called me a fool."

You acted without our sanction. What else would you be?

"I like to think of myself as a free agent," Hodoul said. "If you wanted a slave, you should have put me in the Tree."

Malach leaned closer to the water, swelling to menacing size.

Perhaps you are confused about why we didn't. Do you remember?

"Yes," Hodoul said. "To be a nursemaid to these dregs that it would break the bounds of generosity to call human."

Are you really so obtuse? No, that wasn't your purpose! We have a plan, a timeline. Until we all have the allies we need, we cannot escape, let alone launch our invasion. You were to prepare those we sent you . . .

"Yes, yes." Hodoul waved. "So we can all rule Mysterion

together . . . What you really want is someone to dance when you move your hands. I hate to disappoint you, my friend, but Jack Hodoul is no one's puppet!"

Are you breaking our contract? You realize that comes with consequences?

"You forget that I am a dead man already," Hodoul said. "And dead men are immune to threats. Besides, what would you do if I don't obey? Send a swarm of flies and mosquitoes to irritate me to death?"

The Djinn will not be mocked, Hodoul!

Hodoul smirked. "Oh come on. What's life without a little laughter? As for me, I intend to enjoy myself before they throw my corpse to the sharks. You can find someone else to dance on the end of your strings."

That is being arranged. You won't hear my voice again!

The Djinn vanished, his face cold and furious, and Hodoul was looking down at his own ruined features in the water.

"Somehow," he murmured to himself, "I think that might be too much to hope for."

* * *

Within moments of leaving Hodoul's presence, the Djinn was back over the ocean, winging his way west at an unnatural speed. For several days he followed a direct course, without pausing to rest or eat. He passed over islands but kept his distance, not wanting to take the slightest risk of being spotted. When at last the Brethren islands rose on the horizon, Malach put on an extra burst of speed. He overshot the islands—their habitations deserted—and then turned north toward a patch of low-lying haze in the distance. As he approached, the haze thickened into a bank of smoke. The Djinn pushed in without hesitating. Moments later, the source of the smoke appeared—a ring of fire on the water.

Fearless, the Djinn penetrated the barrier of flames, which licked at him hungrily but left him unscathed. Once through, the storm of the inner waters assaulted and beat at Malach but could not divert him from his course. As he reached the shore, the air turned the consistency of hot soup. Only then did he finally unfold into his natural form, his large tattered wings propelling him on at a more leisurely pace.

The island was little more than a sandbar covered in mangroves. Their last habitation had been luxurious by comparison. After the boy Jonah had destroyed the first Tree, they had been forced to flee, and this had presented itself as the first alternative. But after they had cast the spell to surround the island in the reef of fire, and returned to their natural form, they discovered that the mangrove branches were too frail to hold their weight. They were forced to squat in the swamp mud, an undignified position for any self-respecting Djinn accustomed to looking down on the world from a height.

Regarding the slumped forms of the horde littered across the island, Malach sighed. The loss of the first Tree had set their timeline back. Only his careful husbandry of the new Tree, the special charms he had developed to accelerate its growth, had allowed them to continue the harvest of the Lethes as before.

Still, their progress had been agonizingly slow. The Elder Geist had trusted no one else to harvest the Lethes, and Malach had simply taken up his routine without thinking too much about it. Then that snake Hodoul had thrown everything into disarray, putting the whole endeavor in jeopardy. Unless they could replenish the hosts, and quickly, they would have to start the process of gathering them all over again . . .

Malach wondered, not for the first time, about the risks of his new plan. Was it worth sharing such a noble task with the horde? It might give them the impression that they did not need him, or anyone, to fulfil their destiny. They had seen the Elder Geist torn to pieces. They might get unpleasant ideas for *him* too . . .

But it was too late to think up something else—the horde had become aware of his arrival. Hissing with excitement, they clambered to their feet and into the air, flapping toward him as they hurled questions and demands. Malach ignored them until he reached the center of the island, where the new Tree squatted, an anomalous beast of a baobab beside a pool. An old torn cloak hung from one of the lower branches. As the rest of the Djinn watched with a touch of envy, Malach draped it over himself, and with a touch of theatricality, raised his claws into the air. The hubbub descended into silence.

"The pirate king has rebelled," he said.

The silence persisted as they absorbed the news. They broke into hissing, consternation this time, rising to a high pitch.

"But what of it?" Malach said. "He is not indispensable. Come and look!" He turned away without waiting for them to calm down. From the secret recesses of the cloak, he pulled a pendant, a large chunk of midnight black stone on a chain. Its appearance silenced the horde at once. They crowded forward, jostling each other to watch as Malach swirled the stone in the pool, breaking its surface into ripples.

When the water calmed, an image floated on the surface. A young man with dark skin, oil-black hair and sharp features leaned against the wall made of translucent stone. He stared over a great city, all its building fashioned from the same glass-like material, and the expression on his face was troubled and angry.

"I have already approached him," Malach said, "and he is receptive to us. But even if he fails . . ." He swirled the pendant again. The ripples settled, revealing a tall, athletic woman, very beautiful, with pleated hair piled on her head. She paced back and forth, pausing to look up the face of a granite mountain. "There is always that one. And if *she* fails, there's always someone else. Do you see my point?" he said, looking around at them. "They are *humans*. They have always been susceptible and weak, and they still are. We are Djinn, pure and true as fire. We prevailed once, and we will prevail again!"

Hisses of appreciation punctuated Malach's words. They filled him with confidence. "Now," he said. "The time has come for a change of plan. I must go back out and make arrangements to bring our harvest back." They looked at each other, disappointed. Malach went on quickly, "While I am gone, as a reward for your faithfulness to our cause, I will grant each and every one of you the power to descend to the Lethes and continue the harvest on your own!" They broke into ululations of excitement. "Work hard and we will soon have the bodies we need to escape our confinement!"

The horde could not be contained after that. They elbowed and shoved and clawed each other to wade into the pool. As Malach chanted, they touched the pendant in his claws, each dissolving into the waters.

When the last had vanished, Malach stared into the pool, smiling as he savored the victory. He draped the pendant over his head, closed his eyes, and collapsed into his insect form. This time, he decided on the form of a mosquito. Moments later, the reef of fire disappeared behind him into the bank of smoke. With a single-mindedness quite unnatural for any mosquito, Malach made a bee-line for the west.

Chapter Eight

Several days later, as the sun descended toward the sea, *La Justice* dropped anchor at the Elder's Island. Skiffs drove in toward the beach, where the crews had gathered to greet the king. The four princes waited down near the breaker line. Even from where he sat at the tiller of the lead boat, Disagree could tell from how they stood that they would rather be anywhere else in Mysterion than their current location.

Hodoul's prediction all those years ago had proven itself correct—the captains had returned to parlay when the last of their Claw supplies ran out, their crews on the verge of mutiny. After a long series of delicate negotiations, it came down simple exchange: loyalty and obedience for the title of "prince" and a regular supply of Claw from the king's stores. Something like peace had ensued.

The king murmured over his shoulder, so only Disagree could hear. "They have their men in the trees . . . Didn't I say she has been up to no good while we were gone? We have our work cut out for us, I'm afraid."

Disagree's face remained impassive. "You try to fix things with her?" he said.

Hodoul sighed. "Somehow I think it will take more than a bag of gold and a bouquet of flowers to fix things this time."

The skiff surfed into the beach. As they ran aground, the king leaped onto the sand. A cheer went up, but only from the crews that were loyal to the king. The princes' men watched in hostile silence. Hodoul lifted his hat, waved, and then strode up to where the princes waited, with Disagree a step behind.

They didn't come down to him, Disagree thought. This was bad news all around.

Madame Razor stood at the center of the group, the other three princes behind her.

Once again, Disagree thought, *she has them in their places.*

She spread her arms, smiling. Disagree knew that smile—calculated to disarm, just before she tried to stick a knife between your ribs. "Well my love, there you are," she cried. "I thought you ran away forever!"

"My dear," Hodoul said, bowing low and gesturing with just a little too much theatricality. "I would never dream of running away from you, mostly because I would have turn my back on you to do so."

The princes tittered, Le Moray covering his mouth with one hand while Dubois swayed and Torteau shuffled his feet.

Madame Razor rounded on them. "You like that, do you?"

Their laughter subsided into an uneasy silence under her baleful stare. She turned back to Hodoul. "You turned your back on me when you left to chase your little girl. I'm surprised you didn't fall off the Edge."

Hodoul raised an eyebrow. "I am not sure what you are implying, my dear, but it is inaccurate, not to mention inappropriate for a man my age. If I were to guess, I might say that you were bitter about the past . . ."

"For ten years you were master over me," Madame Razor declared. "But that's done. Now I'm the only one in charge of me."

Le Moray coughed. Madame Razor glanced back. "I'm getting there!" She turned back to Hodoul. "The princes and I have had a little *tête-a-tête*, and we have decided that you had your chance. Now it's our turn."

Hodoul glanced at Disagree. *Of course,* the glance said. *What else?*

"Oh dear!" Hodoul pressed a hand to his heart. "What are you saying to me?"

"We decided on a new arrangement," Madame Razor said. "Something a little more *democratic.* All of us together."

"*Egalité,*" Le Moray said in a wistful voice. "What a beautiful thought!"

Madame Razor threw him a *shut your mouth* look. Le Moray stiffened and fell silent.

"We all vote on everything," she said. "Majority rules!"

Hodoul said nothing.

"Why are you smiling like a *couyon*?" Madame Razor said. "You think this is funny?"

"A little," Hodoul admitted. "You seem to have forgotten that all of your crews together still do not outnumber mine . . ." He paused, seeing the smile spread on Madame Razor's face. "Ah, but I see you know something I do not. Let me guess. You have managed to persuade some of my men with your charms."

Madame Razor laughed. "Between your age and my beauty, what choice is there?"

"True enough," Hodoul said. "But as you may recall, only one of us has an inexhaustible supply of dragon's claws. Let me assure you again that I won't give up my little secrets, even if you took days to skin me alive."

"We need you," Madame Razor said. "But you need us too.

We are more than just indentured servants with titles."

Hodoul raised one shoulder in a lopsided shrug. "What can I say, my dear? You seem to have arranged things. And if the alternative is that we would now turn against each other, throwing away what I must say has been a very profitable peace . . . What choice do I have? If you think that we can work together in harmony . . ." he spread his arms wide in a magnanimous gesture, "then what else can I do except lend my wholehearted support to your proposal? If I could make one small amendment, however . . ." he raised one finger and his face took on an unusually pleading expression.

Madame Razor leaned back with her hands on her hips, her eyes narrowed. "What? What tricks are you up to this time?"

Disagree was wondering the same thing. How on earth was the king going to get out of this one? When the princes couldn't amass the men they needed to outnumber him in a full-frontal attack, it had been easy to keep them in their places. Now that they had the numbers, how could he gain the advantage?

"You wound me, my dear," Hodoul said. "You were always good at that. No, I simply want to ensure that this new democratic alliance is truly . . . democratic. I would hate to see us vote three against two, and then have us divided against each other. I have worked too hard to see that happen again . . ." he paused, recalling something that must have been unpleasant. "I suggest therefore that we work for complete *unanimity* in all our decisions. If even one among us should reject a course of action, the matter will be tabled for further discussion." He raised his voice so that it carried to the crowd behind them. "Whatever we do, let us do it together, or not at all. Equality for one and all!"

The crews had become restless, unable to hear what the

princes and the king were talking about. Now they broke into a cheer. This time, Disagree noticed that the princes' men added their voices to the cheering.

The three princes exchanged glances, as if Hodoul had given them an escape. Madame Razor greeted the announcement with hands on her hips and her lips drawn into a tight line as she regarded Hodoul with glittering eyes. Disagree could imagine what she was thinking. She had planned on forcing the other princes to vote with her, so no matter what Hodoul did, he would always find himself on the losing end. Now he could disrupt any plan she proposed with his vote alone. She had to find some way to get a handle on things without appearing as if she were trampling on the freedom that all the Brethren loved, even if they were all just slaves to Claw and gold and rum . . .

"What a nice proposal," she said as the cheering died down. She cast her gaze around, at the princes and the crowd behind them, but somehow never seemed to take her eyes off Hodoul. "Our dear king is a man who believes in our Brotherhood. Let's hope, my dears, that we can all live up to his expectations!

"Now," she continued. "Enough talk. We have waited here for three months, and those cursed slaves are still holed up on their mountaintop, safe behind their miserable lamp. We are tired of getting fat watching coconuts fall. What plan does the king have to restore our honor and lead us to victory?"

The crews were voluble in their agreement. Although Disagree stayed silent, he too hoped the king would have an answer. On the voyage back from the Falls, Hodoul had spoken little about what he intended to do when they got back to the island. Indeed, he had curtailed his habit of thinking out loud in Disagree's presence—a sign of his new distrust. The rebuff troubled Disagree, but he had resigned himself that Hodoul would never understand how he could help Isabella escape and still consider himself the king's most loyal servant.

"In fact," Hodoul said, "Monsieur Disagree and I do have something of a plan."

Disagree started slightly. What plan?

The king gestured inland. "If you will indulge me?"

"Of course," Madame Razor said. "Lead the way."

"Why don't we walk side by side?" Hodoul suggested. "As a sign of our new fraternity?"

"Very well," Madame Razor said. She strode toward the head of the beach, Hodoul matching her step. The other three princes fell in dutifully on either side of them. Disagree brought up the rear.

"As if I would ever let any of you walk behind me," the king murmured.

"You are wise, my love," Madame Razor murmured back. "You should also learn how to sleep with your eyes open . . ."

The crowd of Brethren parted before them, then followed as they entered the forest. A narrow path wound up among the trees, always climbing. The air was heavy with the smell of rotting mangoes and resounded with birdsong. Within minutes the princes were winded and fell behind. By contrast, Madame Razor maintained her driving pace, while Hodoul seemed untouched by the heat. Disagree, his black skin shining, climbed upwards like an active volcano rising out of the sea.

At last the forest gave way to an expanse of lichen-encrusted granite, with scrub bushes pushing through the cracks and narrow dirt paths winding upwards along the slope. Beyond them, the rock rose in a vertical face crisscrossed with cracks and ledges, somewhere among which was a path to the top. At the moment, the summit itself was enveloped in a thick billowing cloud, tinged by the setting sun.

Madame Razor paused here with hands on hips, panting. "No point going any further."

Disagree craned his head upward. Somewhere up there an ornate lamp was all that stood between them and the People of the Wind, and yet Disagree knew that it was barrier enough. He could still recall with perfect clarity the evening when that fool Guillotine had tried to charge ahead and break through; a searing flash later, nothing had remained of him but a cloud of ash billowing in the evening air.

"We sent scouts every which way," Madame Razor said. "North, south, east, and west. In the dead of night. It didn't matter which way they went or when, it got them. I lost more than twenty good men that way."

"You'd think the lesson would be learned after you lost two or three," Hodoul said.

Madame Razor rounded on him. "At least I was doing something, not running some fool errand at the Edge of the world!"

Hodoul started to reply. Disagree pointed. "Look," he said, and something in his voice commanded their attention.

Around the summit, the cloud had parted, revealing a crowd gathered along the edge of the cliff. In their midst, the lamp hung on a post—ornate and bulbous and gleaming almost too brightly. Beside it stood an old man with charcoal skin and silver hair, and to his left, a slight, sharp-faced man. But only the girl held Disagree's attention, the girl whose tangled blonde hair Disagree had last seen lit up by the lantern on the aft deck as she drove the tyrant's schooner over the Falls of Mysterion.

Chapter Nine

From the edge of the plateau, Isabella stared down at Disagree. Although he stood behind Hodoul, the pirate king faded into the periphery of her vision, a menacing specter from a life she had left behind when she drove Jonah's ship over the Falls of Mysterion. The princes of the Brethren were blurred and undefined on either side of Hodoul, like the edges of an old photograph. Only Disagree loomed sharp and immense. Even from this distance, she imagined every detail of his features from her memories, which now crowded back into her mind out of the darkness into which he had faded.

Tears rose behind her eyes. She took a deep breath to steady herself. The last thing she wanted was for Dio to notice. If he knew what she was feeling, it would only give him the fuel he needed to question her loyalty.

"I told you, didn't I?" Dio cried, gesturing. "I told you we should have made a break for it before. Now that *he's* here, he will put steel in their back, and they will resist us to their last man. Now it's hopeless!"

"Peace, Dio," Pierre said, raising his hand. "We made a decision to wait until Jonah returns. And he *will* return."

"*You* made that decision," Dio said, gesturing at Isabella, "based on the word of a little girl barely unburied!"

"I take wisdom wherever I can find it," Pierre said. "From

the old and the young. We did not have the power to take on the Brethren, even without Hodoul. They would destroy us, and everything the Elder did would be undone. While we have the Lamp," he gestured at where it gleamed, reflecting the setting sun, "we are safe and protected. Jonah promised to return and he will deliver us from the siege."

"So, that's it then," Dio demanded, "hide behind the Lamp and sleep under a tree until someone comes to save us?"

"Yes," Pierre said simply.

"That's what cowards do," Dio said. "And I am not a coward!"

"Well, you will have to put up with a little cowardice until Jonah returns."

"We'll see," Dio said, folding his arms.

"No," Isabella said. "We won't see. You'll do as Pierre says, or pack it up, go down, and parlay with the Brethren—"

"Isabella," the old man said, putting a hand on her arm. "Please stay at peace. The pirate king has something to say."

Below, Hodoul had stepped forward, looking up. The coldness of his eyes reached Isabella even from this distance.

His voice rose up, cold and cordial. "So good to see you again, Isabella. Unfortunate that you are now so far away . . ."

"I am the Regent Elder," Pierre interrupted with a clarity and strength that surprised Isabella. "You can speak with me!"

"Are you sure?" Hodoul said. "No one holding your strings?"

"What do you want, Hodoul?" Pierre shouted. "Speak your piece!"

"Very well," Hodoul said. "The princes and I . . ." he glanced back, ignoring the hostility from Madame Razor, ". . . have decided *unanimously* that we wish to negotiate a peaceful end to this siege. We invite you to send one of your sla—that is, someone to meet us under a flag of truce and parlay terms of peace."

"My instructions are to wait here under the protection of the Lamp until the Elder Jonah returns," Pierre said. "We have enough provisions to last us a lifetime. Why should we trust you and leave our sanctuary?"

"Any place you cannot leave, even a paradise, is nothing more than a prison," Hodoul said. "Is that the life you want for your children and grandchildren, a beautiful prison? If so, by all means. We can last here forever. This island and all the others of Inner Mysterion are ours now. You can stay on your little mountaintop and rot, or we can talk about releasing you to go wherever else you please!"

Dio stepped forward. "Never! We'll fix you or die, you filthy pirate!"

Pierre rounded on him. "Will you keep peace, Dio. This is not the moment!"

"You can't shut me up, old man!" Dio said. "If you don't defend the People, I will!"

Hodoul voice floated up, sounding amused. "It seems, old fellow, you may not speak for everyone after all!"

"I have my instructions from Jonah himself, Hodoul," he said. "And there will be no negotiating them!"

"Yes, but does he not lead with the approval of his people? Do they not declare that he is worthy? What would they say now? He turned tail and ran months ago, and has not returned. My guess is, he is somewhere among the other races of Mysterion by now . . ." Isabella flinched. With unerring instinct, Hodoul had pinpointed the People's single greatest anxiety—that Jonah had abandoned them. Dio's face, etched with loathing at the sight of the Brethren, now radiated with triumph, as if he had been vindicated.

Hodoul continued with relentless calm. "Call me simplistic, but it looks to me like your so-called Elder has decided to make his own way, and you're on your own. Perhaps it is time for your people to decide who is *really* worthy to be your Elder. From the looks of it, they aren't so confident about that anymore."

"You can try to sow as much discord as you wish," Pierre said, with a nervous glance at Dio. "I would expect no less of you. But we are the People of the Wind, and as many opinions as we have, we have one heart!"

"Well, perhaps you should make sure of that," Hodoul said. "We will give you a full day to talk it over. Tomorrow afternoon at this time you can send someone of your choosing to parlay with us, or else we can continue as we have been, and you can die up there waiting for your non-existent Elder to return."

"We don't need time—"

"Until tomorrow!" Hodoul turned away, and he and the princes disappeared into the forest. Disagree paused and then turned to follow. Desperate words crowded to Isabella's lips. She just managed to stop them escaping, but still reached out to prevent him from leaving. Dio saw the gesture. He stared at her a moment, bewildered. Then realization dawned, and he pointed an accusing finger at her.

"You see that?" he cried.

Pierre, who was walking away, turned back. "Now what?" he sighed.

"She reached out her hand, like she was waving!" Dio said.

"I did not see anything," Pierre said.

"She did," Dio insisted. "I saw it!"

Pierre examined Isabella's face. "What happened, Isabella?"

Isabella did not answer. She could no longer restrain the

emotion. Tears broke out and spilled down her cheeks.

"You see?" Dio said. "Her face tells it all. She's in with those scum! That's why she wants us to wait, saying the Elder is coming. To keep us quiet and stuck on this mountain while they eat up our world!"

"That's not true," Isabella whispered, but Pierre's face was heavy with sorrow. Beside him, Shantih's eyes were wide.

"How could it be?" she whispered. "You were unburied . . ."

"It's not true," Isabella repeated.

Dio sensed his advantage. "I claim that this girl is not of the Lamp. I challenge her to submit to the ordeal of Windfire. And just in case any of you accuse me of false judgements, I also will submit myself. You say I should go to the Brethren," he said to Isabella. "Now we'll see who belongs where!"

Chapter Ten

odoul lay on his back against the cushions. His eyes were closed, and his face serene. A book lay open on his chest. The darkness was almost complete, broken only by the open tent flaps, which revealed a clear and starry sky beyond. The breaking of waves was a soft rhythmic hiss-and-suck over the sand outside.

The king and princes had decreed a feast to celebrate the new terms of their alliance. In a demonstration of generosity, they had opened several kegs of rum and issued bags of Claw to all. Crowded at trestle tables, they had gorged themselves on roasted fish and fruit, then danced reels to the fiddlers' tunes as the air had turned thick and acrid with the Claw smoke. It wasn't until well past midnight that the music died away and the final drunken murmurs subsided into a Claw-induced stupor.

There was a soft scuffling sound outside, followed by a groan, and a thump. Hodoul's eyes stayed closed. He didn't move. As shadow blotted out the stars, he rolled away with uncanny speed as a dagger plunged into the pillow where his head had rested. He grabbed the assassin's wrist. "You took your time my dear," he said, twisting Madame Razor's arm up into a half nelson and pinning her against the cushions with his knee in the small of her back. "Sunrise is just a couple of hours away."

Madame Razor struggled, hissing like a cat and cursing him.

"Oh, come now, Natalie," he said. "Why must we squabble like this? A glorious destiny lies ahead for both of us."

"You have a glorious destiny for yourself," Madame Razor panted. "I'm just there to rub your feet at the end of the day!"

"You are unjust," Hodoul said, in a wounded tone. "We were always equals, you and I. And we could have shared the throne years ago, if you hadn't been so stubborn about your damned independence . . ."

"Your crown is too big for anyone's head but yours," Madame Razor said. "Besides, I like sailing my own ship . . ." She continued to struggle, fighting for breath. If he gave for an instant, she would attack him again.

"I need you, Natalie," he said softly. "I have needed you all these years."

"Nice words again! What about that little girl you chased all the way to the Falls, eh?"

"That again? I believed she was one of my descendants among the Lethes. I thought she could be a daughter to me . . ."

"And now she is turned to the tyrant's side, you want me instead."

"No," Hodoul said, with a touch of regret. "I understand that some things cannot be undone. All I ask is that we sail our ships together, side by side, for a while. I promise that when we part courses, we will each be more powerful than ever before. We can divide the world between us. What do you say?"

For the first time, she hesitated. Her struggling lost its intensity.

"Why did you offer to parlay with the slaves?" she said.

"It's the only way to end the siege," Hodoul said.

"You don't really intend to let them go peacefully, do you? If you do, you're a fool—"

"Of course not!" Hodoul said. "Now, can we please . . ."

"So, why give them time? Why go through the motions?"

"Because discord is like yeast," Hodoul said. "It needs time to spread."

Another silence followed, but she had stopped fighting.

"In the future, you make a decision like that without me," Madame Razor said, "and you won't wake up from sleep."

"Agreed," Hodoul said. "Do we have an accord?"

"We do. Now get off me, damn you!"

He relinquished her wrist and rolled off her. She sat up, nursing her arm and wincing.

"What about the other three?" Hodoul said. "They could be a problem . . ."

"Never mind them," Madame Razor said. "My best knives already took care of them. We'll resolve it in the morning."

* * *

Hodoul waited until she was gone before emerging from his tent. The sentries were slumped over. He wasn't sure if she had finished them or just knocked them out, but it didn't matter either way. The other three princes would offer a handy explanation for everything, and they were beyond caring by now.

The darkness had already turned luminous in the east. Dawn was closing in. Madame Razor had indeed taken her time, much longer than Hodoul had anticipated. He didn't have long—an hour at most—and he hurried up the beach and into the forest. Disagree had kept watch at the base of the mountain, in case the slaves tried any treachery.

Hodoul had known the real reason. If he was right, he could ensure that Disagree would play his part without hesitation.

He emerged from the forest at the base of the mountain. His heart raced at the exertion, and the breeze chilled the sweat on his skin. Above, the peak was clear against the stars. He could not make out Disagree. Then something like a boulder in the shadows nearby rose up. "Who goes there?"

"It is the king," Hodoul said. "Stay at ease."

Disagree waited to sit until Hodoul made himself comfortable against a tree and got to work filling his pipe. Once it was lit, the king puffed for a while, saying nothing. Disagree fixed his eyes on the mountaintop again, but his muscles were tensed now, waiting. Since the Falls, the king never came to him unless he had a reason. Not like in the past, when he had sought his company just so he could talk.

What comes now, he wondered.

Disagree had been thinking about Bella. Was she up there, looking down as he kept watch below? More likely she was asleep, frowning in that way of hers. And Disagree recalled how when she belonged to the Brethren, he had often come back from keeping watch on the camp to find her asleep at his door, curled up to keep warm, her forehead creased as if trying to answer some question in her dreams . . .

When he first saw her at the edge of the cliff, he was surprised at his equanimity. Somehow, he had known that she would return to Mysterion. When he brought down the hatchet and sent her ship over the Falls, he had felt that calm conviction. How she would return he did not understand at time. All he had known then was that she had found the answer to the question she had been asking in her sleep. And now he was certain that her journey had come to its end at last up on the mountain.

And yet, another part of himself seethed like lava beneath the surface of his mind, grieving the distance between them. Yes, Bella had found the resting place of her heart, but still the other will within him wanted her to sit beside him again, as they had so many times before. As the king grew ever more distant, he wanted back the only friendship he had ever known, strange and unlikely as it was.

"They won't agree to parlay, of course," Hodoul said, his tone confiding in a way that Disagree hadn't heard in a while. "That's obvious. They won't leave their stronghold willingly. We will have to draw them out . . ."

He was silent. Disagree sensed the king wanted him to respond, but resisted the urge. *This time he comes to* me.

"You were right," Hodoul continued at last. "I had a weakness for her. I believed in her, and I hoped for much—too much perhaps. You know what I wanted. A place at my side. In time, she would inherit the throne . . ."

Again, he paused. Disagree could feel his eyes, but did not turn to meet them.

"But she was deceived," Hodoul said. "And too stubborn to see her own folly. What she did was traitorous, but remember . . ." He lowered his voice to a whisper. "Only you and I know the truth of that, Disagree."

"I remember you said that to me," Disagree said. "No one else saw my treason too."

Hodoul waved impatiently. "Forget all that. I never really doubted you. Your misplaced compassion, perhaps, but not your loyalty. Now I need you more than ever. I need you to help me win Isabella back."

Disagree turned and stared into the shadow pits that were the king's eyes. He wanted to believe him. A force within, almost irresistible, compelled to push aside everything else he knew and just believe.

"If we—if *you* can convince her," the king said. "Help her see her mistake. She could be a great Queen. If we could just show her the greatness of the destiny that awaits, we can begin again, just as you and I have . . ."

Disagree said nothing. He turned and stared up at the mountaintop, now turning red in the face of the dawn. He thought he could see figures moving near the lamp, which glowed even now like an ancient star.

"You have a plan?" he said at last.

"Yes," Hodoul said. "But I need your help with it."

Disagree turned back to him. His eyes burned with a hidden fire. "I help you, even when you think I do not."

At that moment, a blinding explosion lit up the mountaintop. Arcs of fire snaked out from the spot where the lamp had been, the golden radiance of the sunrise falling back before the brilliance of those flames.

"The fire," Disagree said. "The fire of the lamp."

Chapter Eleven

s the sun broke over the edge of the ocean, the People of the Wind emerged from their lean-tos and trickled down toward the Lamp-post. There, Dio and Isabella faced each other. Between them, Pierre was frailer than ever. Since before dawn, he had been trying to convince Dio to withdraw the challenge.

He tried once more. "Please consider, Dio. Isn't it enough that she struggled to kindle the Lamp, as you did?"

"You saw her!" Dio repeated, for the third time. "She was reaching out to her friends. We need to know whether the Djinn have been whispering in her ear. Who knows? Maybe they've turned her back to her old loyalties!"

The People murmured in fearful agreement. Nearby, Shantih clung to one of the women, her eyes wide, sorrowful. Isabella wished she could have explained to the little girl about Disagree. It was too late now.

Perhaps afterwards, she thought. *If I survive . . .*

She had avoided returning to the camp to eat the night before. She hadn't even tried to sleep. Instead, she followed the edge of the cliff, circumnavigating the plateau more times than she could count, pausing only when the strain of fiddle reel or a drunken shout floated up from somewhere below. Then the image of Disagree's face had floated back into her mind from the darkness to which she had tried to banish it. She shook her head, as if to dislodge the vision, and continued her restless circuit of the plateau.

Had it all been for nothing? Had she jumped off the Edge of the world, only to find that she did not belong, even here?

Pierre was addressing everyone. "The Elder destroyed the Djinn Tree. The Djinn are gone from Mysterion . . ."

Dio regarded him with a crooked smile. "If you believe they are gone, then where is the Higher Mysterion? Why are the Brethren here? No, old man, the Djinn are hidden, but they are still working," he turned on Isabella and pointed, "and their servants are also well concealed. But I trust my guts, and my guts tell me that *she* is not to be trusted, and I am willing to put my own life to the test to prove it!"

"Enough talk," Isabella said. "Pierre, if this fool wants to test me, I'm ready for a test. Let's just get it over with."

"Please . . ." Pierre's voice quavered. "Both of you . . ."

"Let's do it!" Isabella said. If she had to wait any longer, something would give. She had to know once and for all where she belonged.

"Yes," Dio said. "Get on with it, old man." He was sweating. In the crowd, a baby wailed. Despite the mother's efforts, its cries rose, growing more frantic. The mother hurried away. The cries faded.

Pierre's shoulders slumped at last. "I told the Elder that I was just an old fisherman. I told him this was not for me . . ." He reached up and took the Lamp down from the post with both hands. He held it up, radiant in the rising sun. "So be it!" His voice rose, now firm and steady. "He gave me the right to hold the Lamp without enduring Windfire, but anyone else who would reach for it must first be purified. If they truly belong to the Lamp, they will survive. If not, if their hearts are corrupted . . ."

He did not finish the sentence, but held the Lamp out to Dio and Isabella. The crowd pressed forward, their faces both fascinated and terrified. They had seen what the Lamp had done to the Brethren scouts who had tried to find their way onto the plateau and were now nothing but scattered ashes in the wind.

They had not been of the Lamp—that much was clear.

Feeling the press of the crowd behind, feeling the weight of their stares, Isabella closed her eyes and took a deep breath. If she survived, and Jonah *had* run to find refuge in the Outer Mysterion, with the Solitaries . . . Perhaps he couldn't find a way to save them, so rather than face them again, he had run . .

.

What then? She shook her head. *Focus, idiot. This is just the sort of thinking that will get you burned to a crisp!*

Dio misunderstood her movement. "Backing out? Not unless you admit you have turned your back on the Wind!"

Isabella looked at him. Holding his eyes, she stepped forward. The Lamp brightened, sensing her approach. Pierre's hands shook, his eyes blurred with grief at what might happen in a moment. Isabella took another step forward. Her heart drummed against her chest. She narrowed her eyes as the Lamp's intensity now rivalled the brilliance of the sunrise. Isabella took a deep breath and held it, as if about to dive to the bottom of the ocean. She reached forward with one hand, and touched the surface.

A rope of blinding flame spun out through the grillwork and encircled her, binding her head to foot. Like the points of hot wires, the flames worked their way through her skin, into her veins and up into her heart. Her heartbeat seemed to have lost all rhythm, racing and slowing all at once. Dio's pale face, the terrified faces of the crowd around them, melted and ran in her vision like liquid glass. Everything flickered, went out, flashed before her, then vanished, plunging her into darkness.

She was somewhere else now—a place she knew too well—no longer standing, but lying on a mattress that smelled like old sweat. The only light in the room emanated from the outline of the door.

In the living room, her father's voice, loud and slurred. "What now? What is the little vixen doing this time, eh?"

Her mother, then, in a self-pitying whine. "She never listen to me. I ask her where she been, she tell me none of my business, and why don't I pour myself another drink! No respect for her mother who gave her life . . ."

"You don't know where she was? Where do you think she was? With that lay-about down at la boutique!"

"She won't listen . . .. After all we do . . ."

"Not you, perhaps. Useless! But I tell you something—she listen to me!"

His footsteps beat down the hallway. His feet blocked the light under the doorway. He pounded. The door shivered.

"Let me in!"

Isabella stood.

"Open this door!" he shouted.

Any moment now, he would kick it in. Isabella could feel the threads of Windfire working their way into her heart, starting to burn. She knew what she had to do, but she wanted something else. And the knife was under her pillow, waiting to do the same bloody work it had done in countless nightmares.

The Windfire was catching now, the pain intensifying and beginning to spread through her arteries. She had to do it . . .

Just breathe, Jonah's voice said. And Disagree's face floated back again. He nodded and smiled, and she knew at that moment that he would never be lost to her. Even in Mysterion, he would stand at her back.

She took a deep breath and exhaled, her breathing continuing beyond the capacity of her lung. Her feet unlocked. She went the door and opened it, catching her father in mid pound. For a moment, he gaped in surprise. The scene dissolved, burned away by the Windfire that swept through her, burning but no longer consuming, a flame pure and bright and painless. Pierre's face reappeared, his tired features relieved and joyful for the first time in weeks; then Dio, his pale face even paler with dismay; and finally, the crowd and the green plateau and the sky red and gold in the first rays of the sun.

The nightmare was over. Never again would she be forced to face that moment. She belonged to the Wind forever.

She stepped away from the Lamp in the hush of the crowd. They had seen her enveloped in Windfire and remain not only unscathed, but the hunger of her features had vanished, leaving her luminously beautiful.

She turned her eyes to Dio and spoke, surprised at her own lack of bitterness toward him. "Your turn."

Dio swallowed, sweating, his Adam's apple bobbing. His eyes darted from side to side, looking for another way out. But the crowd pressed close in on either side. There was nowhere to go but toward the Lamp or down the narrow path to the bottom of the mountain and the Brethren encampment.

He gathered himself, squared his shoulders, and nodded. "According to my oath," he said, in a slightly hoarse voice. Taking a deep breath, he took a step toward the Lamp. He hesitated, reached out, and took another step. The Lamp flared up, anticipating his touch. With the tips of his fingers within an inch of the Lamp, Dio hesitated so long, the crowd grew restless.

"Do you wish to retract?" Pierre said.

Dio came back from far away. He looked around one last time and for the first time, Isabella felt sorry for him.

"You don't have to," she said. "You have been unburied, and that's good enough."

The words seemed to galvanize him. A flash of resentment crossed his face.

"I don't need your charity," he said. He grabbed at the Lamp.

With a roar like a rushing wind, the rope of flame encircled him until he was no longer visible beneath the fire. At first, he was quiet, twitching as the threads of light worked their way into him. Then he began to moan, a sound that soon rose into a scream, drawing out until it was unbearable to hear. The crowd broke up and scattered, half-running away across the plateau, not turning to look back, parents holding their children close, covering their ears and eyes so that they wouldn't look. Pierre's face was a grim rictus, aging as he held the Lamp. Isabella too wanted to run, but she knew she could not abandon Pierre; she had to see it through to the end. It could not be long in coming . . .

Dio's scream ended with a single shriek, "Leave me alone!" The Windfire around him exploded in a blinding flash. Dio was gone, his ashes drifting off in the evening air. As if someone had turned off a switch, the Lamp went out. Pierre held it for a moment, stunned. He turned as if in a trance and hung it back on its post. Then all his strength went out of him. He swayed, and would have collapsed if Isabella had not run forward to catch him.

She lowered him onto a rock. He shivered in her arms, as if in a high fever.

"It's too much," he muttered. "I told him . . ."

"It's over now," Isabella said.

"I am not an executioner," Pierre said. His eyes pleaded up at her.

"You did not kill him," Isabella said. "His heart turned back to the Lethes, and the Lamp knew it. He lost himself."

Pierre shook his head. "Some things are just too heavy. I cannot do that again."

"You won't have to," Isabella said. "Jonah will return."

"Are you sure?" Pierre said. "How do you know?"

Isabella looked down at him. "Because the Wind told me he will."

Chapter Twelve

Just after noon, the king and Madame Razor, along with Disagree and a few crewmen and women (deemed trustworthy because they were still conscious and mostly sober), went down the beach in a line, kicking the others out of their rum-and-Claw-induced blackouts. Eventually, they managed to assemble most of the crews, bleary-eyed and heads hanging, in front of a banyan tree at the edge of the forest. The rest, still scattered prone on the sand, were either dead or so comatose that they might as well be dead.

As they arrived at the banyan tree, the crews could not fail to notice the large canvas spread on the sand over three objects that looked suspiciously like bodies. Also curious were the ropes that emerged from under the canvas to hang over the branches of banyan tree. Madame Razor watched them, amused at their puzzled expressions. Judging the moment, she turned her head and nodded. Several crewmen hauled on the ropes, and the objects slid out from under the canvas and rose into the air. There was no doubt they were bodies. There was also no doubt whose bodies they were, despite their swollen, discolored faces.

Madame Razor stepped forward, her eyes roving, settling on those who had belonged to Torteau, Du Bois, and Le Moray. "You all know that the princes and the King had formed a new alliance, based on mutual trust and fraternity. You all heard the pact we made." The crews shifted, a few nods and murmurs of agreement. "Well, I regret to inform you that these three . . ." She pointed at the bodies. "These three had no interest in honoring our alliance. Last night, they conspired to assassinate the King in his tent!" The murmurs rose in pitch. Her and the king's crews were turning on the others, a clatter of swords being drawn. Madame Razor held up her hands. "Peace! For now . . .

"They committed treachery against the King, and now have paid the price for their crimes, as the Code dictates. There is no need for vengeance, because justice has been served. We also believe that they acted alone—they came alone while the rest of you were sleeping—and no one else was involved. None of you have a quarrel, so put up your swords!" She waited until they obeyed before continuing. "To those without a prince I now offer a place on my crew. The King has agreed," she nodded at Hodoul, who inclined his head, "to continue the terms of our former alliance. From this time on, there will be two crews of the Brethren, and he and I together will lead you in harmony. Agreed?"

The crews exchanged glances. Someone called, "If we don't?"

Madame Razor smiled. "Then we will assume that you were complicit in this crime, and you will face the same fate as them."

None of the dead princes' crews hesitated, allowing themselves to be divided evenly between Madame Razor and the king's crews. As they crowded in to sign his log book, Hodoul murmured to Disagree in an undertone, "As you can see, it's easy to rule human beings—when you find the right levers to pull."

The sun was already at half-mast when the last crew member made his mark in the log—an old fellow with a bald head and a scar that cut diagonally across his features, twisting one side of his mouth downward. As he shuffled away, Hodoul lifted his head and raised his voice to carry to all of the Brethren. At his voice, their excited conversations died away and their jostling and milling came to a standstill.

"Now, Brethren, we will complete the task for which we came to this island. We will draw out those miserable slaves from their hilltop fortress and claim the plateau. From here, we will strike out north and south and east and west, conquering wherever we go. But more importantly, we will bring the world under our rule. We will show them what it means to be one of the Brethren. To be truly free!"

The Brethren sent up a roar of approval, frightening flocks of pigeons in the trees.

"Forward!" Madame Razor shouted. Together, she and Hodoul strode up into the forest. Behind them, the Brethren rushed forward like a wave, shoving each other to get ahead. None of them, however, dared overtake the king and Madame Razor, but instead spread out behind them in an arrowhead formation.

Disagree could have outpaced Hodoul, but he was careful to keep one step behind. He had never doubted that the king would even the odds stacked against him, but even he had been surprised at how quickly it had unfolded. What had the king promised Madame Razor in exchange for her loyalty? Probably the same prize he had in store for Isabella. If that was the case, Madame Razor would be useful until Hodoul could pass on to Isabella the destiny he had envisioned for her from the very beginning.

For that, Disagree would follow without question the course of action that the king had laid out the night before. Even in the face of that fire, those great tendrils of light reaching from the lamp to consume him, he would obey Hodoul in the hope she would give him back something he had lost long ago.

But what if . . . And now the other possibility moved like a shark beneath the surface of Disagree's thoughts—so dark that he almost could not bring himself to give voice to it. He gritted his teeth, and forced himself. What if Hodoul was *lying* about his hopes for Isabella? What if he wanted nothing more than to use Disagree to lure her out, and then use her to force the People off the plateau?

The thought broke the surface, thrashing around, as if caught in a net. *If it is true*, Disagree thought, *then I cannot . . .*

And what if he failed? What if the fire reached him before Bella could? The truth was, Disagree could not be certain if Hodoul *had* really forgiven him for the humiliation at the Falls. The outcome of this plan depended on so many unknowns. It was unlike the king, who liked to foresee and forestall every variable. Was the whole thing just his way of punishing Disagree without having to look him in the eyes?

They emerged from the trees at the base of the mountain, the host of the Brethren fanning out on either side along the tree line. At the top of the mountain, the People lined the edge of the cliff, lit up in the late afternoon sun. Disagree spotted Isabella at once, feeling her eyes on him, even from this distance.

"What now?" Madame Razor said.

"Now, my dear," Hodoul said, "we put my plan into action."

"I don't understand," Madame Razor said. "More tricks again? It better not be—"

"No tricks," Hodoul said. "It will become clear in a moment, I promise." He turned to Disagree. "Are you ready?"

A bead of sweat ran down Disagree's face. His heart beat faster. "Yes."

Hodoul must have sensed his hesitation. "She will get to you before it happens," he said. "I am certain of that."

"I know," Disagree said. The voice inside him added, desperate, *But then what?* And still he had no answer . . .

Hodoul nodded. "Good." He stepped forward, lifted his head, his attention fixed on the figure of the old black man and Isabella by his side, and called, "Have you considered my offer, old man? What is your choice?"

The old man's voice floated down to them, faint and quavering. "Our answer is the same as it was yesterday, Hodoul!"

Hodoul threw up his hands. "Very well. I must follow a course I had hoped to avoid." He turned to Disagree. "Go!"

With sweat running down his face, his heart painful in his chest, Disagree took a deep breath and broke into a run, taking the slope in even strides. The Brethren broke into a cheer. Madame Razor grinned, anticipating the destruction that was to come. Hodoul smiled too, but it did not touch his eyes.

The sun lit up the rock-face ahead of Disagree. He could see with great clarity every crack and turn in the path that zigzagged upward to the plateau. But in his mind, he was walking into absolute darkness. He knew that an abyss could gape at any moment beneath him, dropping him into endless night. Or perhaps this was just a sunless gorge, about to open into a place he had never seen before.

All he knew how to do was keep on obeying, and hoping—as he had always done.

Then Isabella's voice, high and terrified, reached down to

him. "Dis, don't do it! The Lamp will destroy you!"

Chapter Thirteen

As she looked down at Disagree, the paralysis of terror took hold of Isabella. She couldn't watch it happen, not to *him* . . . By her side, Shantih grabbed her hand, as if sensing that she might have to hold Isabella back. Pierre looked back and forth, not understanding, his distress evident in the lines of his face.

"Why isn't he stopping?" Isabella whispered. She raised her voice again. "Dis! What are you doing? Please stop!"

Disagree didn't lift his head. He charged at the path without a break in his step, unstoppable. Below, along the tree line, the Brethren roared their encouragement with the voice of single great beast.

The Lamp, which had reflected the rays of the descending sun, now flared with its own radiance. The fire, emanating from somewhere inside the grillwork that joined the base and the cupola-shaped top, intensified with exponential speed. Each step that Disagree took fanned the flame, which as yet took no shape but penetrated the metal itself until the whole Lamp glowed, becoming brighter with every passing moment.

"No," Isabella whispered. She tugged at Shantih, trying to disengage her hand. The little girl tightened her grip.

"Don't go, Bella-Bella!" she said.

Pierre's hand gripped her shoulder. "Listen to her, Isabella.

You are one of the People. We are your family now . . ."

"But so is he!" Isabella said, shrugging off the hand, still struggling to get free of Shantih, who was surprisingly tenacious.

"He's one of the Brethren," Pierre said. "He's the enemy. An enemy of the Lamp. Let it deal with him like the others."

Those words galvanized Isabella. She rounded on the old man. "He is not the enemy! He helped me kindle the Lamp, not just Jonah. And he helped me survive the Ordeal. Do you understand? He's my friend!" She lowered herself level with Shantih, and her voice softened. "Please let me go, little one. This is not the end. The Wind is blowing in this too, I'm sure of it. I need to help my friend now."

Something moved in Shantih's eyes, some realization. She nodded and let go. Isabella kissed her cheek and, without looking back, raced down the path as fast as she dared, leaping down the steep places, from rock to rock. As the sun touched the horizon, the Lamp blazed like a rival sunrise at her back. Below her, Disagree was climbing fast along the path. If she didn't reach him soon, it would be too late.

* * *

The light from above Disagree flooded the side of the mountain, throwing each crevice and crack in the face of the rock into sharp relief. His heart felt as if it had come dislodged and was trying to break out of his chest. A wind breathed down into his face from the plateau, cooling his sweat-drenched skin. He ran on, his sandaled feet slapping on the rock with mechanical regularity, as if someone else were running for him.

"Dis!" Isabella cried from somewhere above him. Again, Disagree forced himself not to look for her, watching the path directly in front of his next step. The certainty about what he had to do had finally come to him.

The brilliance of the lamp had bleached the world white. He felt the earth under his feet, but he no longer knew where he was going. At any moment he might stumble off into the void.

A body collided with his. Disagree looked down into Isabella's tear-stained face.

"Stop," she whispered, clinging to him. "Please stop."

The sadness overwhelmed him. "No. I cannot betray you. I cannot betray him. There is only one way forward."

And he picked her up like a child, and burst into a sprint.

"No!" Isabella screamed.

The light around them shattered. Strands of Windfire arced down from the Lamp. It pierced Disagree through every pore in his skin. He shrieked, as darkness swept over him like a wave, then rushed away.

The mountain had vanished. He stood now on a flat-beaten patch of red earth in front of a long, whitewashed building with a thatched roof. A series of low doors curtained with coir mats repeated down the row.

Behind and on either side, a shadowy silent crowd had gathered, but Disagree did not turn to look at them. His eyes were fixed on the man who stood in front of him, a tall man looming over him (or so he seemed—Disagree had shrunk to the size of a child). The man's name came back to Disagree—the master, Monsieur. His long handsome face was now flushed with anger, his eyes snapping cold.

"Apologize to the Monsieur!"

Disagree's mother stood behind the master at his shoulder, her dark eyes wide with fear.

"Apologize!" she said again. "Apologize! Apologize!"

As she repeated the word over and over with ever greater hysteria in her voice, the master loomed higher and higher over Disagree. Behind him, the crowd of faceless slaves formed a wall, hemming him in.

It had been years since he had experienced the nightmare. Lord Geist had helped him escape from the plantation, from his life as the bastard son of Monsieur De Sagré's concubine. In exchange, Disagree had given himself to the Tree, where he had slept and dreamed this moment again and again. Even after Hodoul came to claim him and most of his former life had faded from his mind, the memory of it was etched deep in his waking moments.

He knew only too well how the nightmare ended, the moment of choice that would bring the darkness flooding over. As the thought of it came to him, the burning of Windfire returned, flooding through his veins, working its way toward his heart. Still, he broke eye contact with Monsieur to look down. The black stone lay waiting for him. All he needed to do was pick it up and throw it, smashing the master's handsome face, throwing him backwards as the women and his mother screamed without words.

Then the nightmare would be over—until it began again.

As Disagree stared down at the stone, its blackness sucked at him, drawing him down with an almost irresistible force. The Windfire had reached his heart, and now radiated out toward his extremities.

"Apologize to the Monsieur!" his mother said.

Disagree wanted to shriek at the pain. Windfire had now filled his entire body, burning him up from the inside out.

Instead, he clenched his jaw, and bent down toward the stone.

Someone said, "Jean."

Disagree knew that voice. Its owner should not be present in this moment, but somehow she was, and the knowledge gave him the strength to break the gravitational pull of the stone. He straightened up. Isabella stood at his side, smiling down. The hungriness he had always known in her face had smoothed. Her hair floated around her head like a cloud in the early morning sunlight. She was beautiful.

"This can end another way," she said.

"Apologize!" His mother sounded desperate.

"Take my hand," Isabella said, reaching out. "And we will walk away."

The Windfire had reached its peak intensity. "It hurts!" he screamed.

"I know," Isabella said. "Take my hand!"

Disagree grabbed her hand—it was the same size as his own, pale against his black skin—and followed as Isabella turned away. Then the flames of Windfire consumed everything. The people gathered around him vanished like shadows in the sunlight. Looking over his shoulder, Disagree caught a glimpse of the master's gaping face, and the fear in his mother's eyes giving way to sadness.

"I love you mama," he called.

She raised her hand to wave, then vanished. Disagree stood once again on the mountain path in the light of the setting sun.

* * *

The blast of Windfire had thrown Isabella to the ground. Now she clambered to her feet, staring at Disagree, uncomprehending.

"You survived," she whispered. "You survived the Ordeal."

Disagree looked at his hands. "Yes," he said, bemused. He raised his eyes. "You were there, Bella. You did it."

Isabella took his hands. "No. It happens in your heart. That's how the Windfire works."

"But you were there," he repeated.

"And *you* were there in my Ordeal," Isabella replied. "You didn't do it, but you gave me strength to let go of the night-mare."

"Yes." Disagree nodded. "The nightmare in the Tree."

"It's over now," Isabella said. "You are one of the People. You're with me and all of us now . . ." She started to cry.

A cloud of compassion filled Disagree's eyes. He looked up to where the People had crowded at the edge of the cliff, staring down at them in nonplussed silence. Then he lowered his gaze to Isabella again.

"Yes," he said. "And also, no."

Isabella gaped at him. "What do you mean? You can't go back to . . . to *him*! The Windfire showed you who he really is . . ."

"I always know who he is," Disagree said. "But I stand by him even so. Now, I know why. Not because I am a slave. Not even because he saved my life years ago and I owe him. Not because any of these things!"

"Then why?" Isabella cried.

"Because it is right," Disagree replied simply. "It is right not to throw the stone, even at someone like him."

Isabella was silent, grief-stricken. She didn't want to accept Disagree's words. After all this time, to see him walk away back down to stand behind that monster would be unbearable. But she too had survived the Ordeal of Windfire, and she could no longer look at the world without seeing it as it really was.

"What about me?" she said at last. "You stood behind me, even when I went back to the Lethes. What about that now?"

Disagree's eyes mirrored her grief. "I still take care of you. That is why you must go back, and stay. And I will go back to the king. He sent me up here to bring you out, to use you for his own purpose. I thought, because of that, I have no choice but to run into the Fire. I cannot betray him, and I cannot betray you . . . But I still live . . ." He raised his hands. "So I must go back until he sends me away forever."

"But . . ." Isabella's eyes widened in horror. "If you go back to him without me . . . He can see us together right now . . ." she gestured at the intent upturned faces of Hodoul and Madame Razor. Around them, the Brethren were silent, waiting, not knowing what had just happened. "If you go back to him without me," she continued. "He will hang you. I mean, I'm surprised he didn't hang you after the Falls!"

"Perhaps," Disagree said. "But I must do it still." He disengaged his hands from her grip. "Now, you go back up."

"No!" She grabbed him again.

"Bella," he said. "I must. Let me go."

"I know you must," Isabella said. "But you are not going without me."

Disagree's eyes widened. "No! I cannot—"

"That's my choice," Isabella cut in. "Just as it is your choice to go down."

"What about your friends?" Dis said. "He will use you to force them out. Think of them!"

Isabella raised her eyes to the anxious faces looking down from the plateau. Among them, only Shantih was serene. The little girl smiled and waved. An odd gesture, but Isabella took a new strength from it.

She turned to Disagree. "They know that you are one of the People. They would never abandon you. And I won't either."

"He wins then," Disagree said. "He wins everything!"

"Not necessarily," Isabella said. "The Windfire has tested us both. Both of us are here because of it. This isn't the end."

Disagree searched her face for wavering. Finding none, his shoulders sagged.

"Come then," he muttered. "Walk in front of me."

Chapter Fourteen

Isabella led the way down the path as the light turned red and faded to a brief dusk. The crews, at first uncertain how to respond to these developments, had now taken up a cheer that rose in volume they closer they came. By contrast, the king and Madame Razor waited in silence. Neither of them was smiling.

Above, the People of the Wind watched them. Their grief was a palpable thing, drawing Isabella back. She clung to the memory of Shantih's little wave to steady herself and take the next step down the path.

They reached the base of the mountain. Moments later, she and Hodoul faced each other, with Disagree at her back.

"I knew you were capable of anything," Isabella said. "I never thought you would go this far. Risking the life of your most loyal servant, who stood by you when you deserved to be abandoned, just to get to me."

"She has some tongue on her, eh?" Madame Razor said. "How about I cut it out?" She stepped forward, but Hodoul raised his hand. His eyes flicked up to Disagree's face before returning to Isabella.

"You are important to me," Hodoul said. "But not as important as you think. Manacles, hands and feet!" he shouted. One of the men came forward with the chains. The king tossed them to Disagree. "Bind her."

Disagree frowned. "She come freely."

The king regarded him, expressionless. "I won't ask again."

Disagree obeyed. Once he had locked the manacles around her ankles, he straightened up. Hodoul waited for him to say something. When Disagree did not oblige, the king turned to Isabella. "There was a time when I would have given—when I *did* give—everything for you. However, you were fool enough to betray me, and as everyone knows, there can be no mercy for betrayers, even remorseful ones."

"I didn't expect mercy," Isabella said. "Though I think Disagree still had hope."

"You lie to me," Disagree said. It was a statement.

"And yet you aren't surprised," Hodoul said.

"No," Disagree replied softly. "I think this was your test. To see if I will obey you even against my own heart."

Hodoul inclined his head. "You would have made a good king. If only you would stop wasting your pity." He grabbed Isabella, drew his dagger and pressed it to her neck. "Bring me a light!" Someone hurried forward, bearing a torch. "Hold it over me," Hodoul commanded. "So the slaves can see us clearly!"

Early evening had veiled the mountaintop in darkness. Hodoul called up, "Are you listening to me, old man?"

After a pause, Pierre's voice, quavering, defeated, floated down. "I am listening."

"I have a simple request. Take up that lamp and bring it down here, by yourself, and throw it into the sea."

The Brethren were stunned into momentary silence. Then a storm of protest rose up.

"Are you crazy?" Madame Razor cried. "He could kill us all!"

"Not with our guarantee," Hodoul replied, indicating Isabella with his head. "Silence!"

The complaints faded away to a lower muttering.

"I cannot," Pierre cried out of the darkness. "I cannot leave the People defenseless!"

"Then I will cut her throat," Hodoul replied. "I am tired of waiting. You have till the count of three. One . . .!"

"Very well!" Pierre shouted—a man who had reached his limit. The sounds of pleading and weeping could be heard from above as a light flared—the Lamp coming to life, illuminating Pierre's woolly white head as he took it down from its post. As he started down the path, the voices rose, plaintive. Without the Lamp, nothing would prevent the Brethren attacking. And no one would survive until morning.

Isabella knew that those voices must be tearing Pierre apart on the inside. Still, the glow of the Lamp continued to work its way back and forth in the darkness as the old man shuffled down like a man condemned to death. As he reached the base, the flame intensified, sensing the presence of enemies in the tree line.

"Clear a path!" Hodoul shouted. "Stand clear and let the old man through!"

The Brethren obeyed with alacrity, shoving each other to open a way through the forest.

Pierre had hesitated at the base of the cliff. "What do you want of me?" he said. The hand holding the Lamp shook.

"Go down to the beach," Hodoul said, still holding Isabella close, with the dagger at her throat. "Take one of the boats you find there and row out beyond the reef, beyond the ships. When you reach the open water, drop the Lamp overboard. We will follow, to make sure. After that, you may row as far as your arms will pull you. Get yourself lost somewhere and pray that we never find you." He stepped back and aside, pulling Isabella with him as he made way for Pierre to pass. "Now, move!"

Pierre's face was stricken. "Throw the Lamp away . . ." he whispered. "It was given to me to protect the People . . ."

"Would you like to test my resolve?" Hodoul said, and he slid the blade lightly across Isabella's neck. She stiffened and gasped and a dark line opened on her pale skin, a trickle of blood from the wound.

"Stop!" Pierre cried. "I will do it!"

Walking as if condemned to death, Pierre followed the path through the trees, the sea of Brethren hanging back several yards on either hand. The Lamp glowed in Pierre's hand, pulsing stronger and weaker to the movement of the crowd. When he was a safe distance away, Hodoul shoved Isabella at Disagree.

"Watch her," he said. "We will dispense a little justice later."

"And you don't try anything either," Madame Razor said to Disagree. "I'll be watching!"

"At last, I am in no doubt of Monsieur Disagree's loyalty, my dear," Hodoul said. "We have nothing to worry about."

"Speak for yourself," Madame Razor said.

The king and Madame Razor hurried away after Pierre, and the Brethren followed in full spate, rowdy and jostling. Elbowed by passing crewmen, and at one point shoved to the ground by one of the women, Isabella soon fell behind, stumbling and tripping in her chains. Disagree followed behind, helping her along when no one was looking. Several yards down the hill, they caught up with the crowd, now hanging back in fear. They couldn't see Pierre ahead, but the Lamp's radiance lit the underside of the trees.

In front, Hodoul shouted, "Keep your distance! Keep back,

you fools!"

They continued at a slower pace, keeping a safe distance behind Pierre. The forest gave way to coconut trees, the soil to white sand. The sea opened before them, the water glittering under the newly-risen moon.

Pierre shuffled over to one of the Brethren's skiffs, pulled up high on the sand. He launched the boat, working her round until her bow pointed into the open ocean. He hauled on the oars, the Lamp resting amidships between his knees. Pierre drove her away across the open water toward the line of the reef and the blockade of Brethren ships.

Hodoul's eyes found Disagree. "Launch a boat. Bring her too," he indicated Isabella, "in case he needs motivating."

Disagree lifted Isabella into a nearby boat. He shoved off, and Hodoul clambered in.

"Will you join us, my dear?" the king asked Madame Razor.

She dismissed him with a wave. "Go and finish it. I will organize these dogs of ours, so they are ready to attack."

"Excellent," Hodoul said. "They will all need torches. That path is treacherous—"

"I know my business," Madame Razor snapped. "You take care of yours. Especially her—" she narrowed her eyes at Isabella. "While you're at it, why not cut her throat and sink her with that damned lamp?"

Hodoul inclined his head. "As you say, we should take care of our own business. Full ahead," he said to Disagree.

They pulled swiftly away from the shore as Madame Razor shouted orders, and men scattered in every direction to obey. Pierre had passed through the reef, the line of the blockade, and into open ocean.

"Faster," Hodoul said. "Get within hailing distance."

Disagree obeyed. He drove them through the reef, the surf pounding around as the hull bucked and tossed. They cut the blockade between a Dhow and a clipper. Pierre came into view a league ahead, still rowing.

Hodoul stood and shouted, "That's far enough, old man!"

Pierre paused. He pulled the oars in and stood, framed against the dark sky, his white hair lit up by the moon.

Hodoul dragged Isabella to her feet and put the knife to her throat. "Throw it in!"

The old man reached down for the Lamp and held it up before him. His voice, low and haggard, floated to them on the wind. "Jonah gave me care of this Lamp. I will not throw it and run. I go wherever it goes."

Isabella started to squirm and struggle, her face contorting. "Pierre!" she screamed. "No!"

Pierre stepped onto the gunwale. The boat tipped, and he dropped in almost without a splash. He did not resurface.

Disagree turned back to face the king as Isabella fought and screamed.

"You kill her now, too?" Disagree said.

Hodoul's eyes met his, calm as ever. "And if I did?"

"You test me again?" Disagree said. "How many tests before you trust me?"

"As many—" Hodoul said, then stopped. He looked up, narrowed his eyes. Disagree turned to follow the look.

Two lights had risen above the horizon. They resembled stars, except swelling, moving toward them at a high speed. There was something about the way they flickered that Disagree had seen before . . . He tried to place the memory, but couldn't. Then Isabella, who had grown quiet, spoke into the silence.

"The Angeli," she whispered. "He's come back!"

III

Part Three

Chapter Fifteen

L ike a flock of migrating frigate birds, a host of Angeli floated east over the turbulent golden surface of Okean. Their eyes were fixed, as always, on the surface. And, as always, the objects of their attention were invisible to human eyes. Only the Angeli could see the rough arrowhead of the Mezoramian fleet of hover-ships right below, down to the gleaming solar sails and the trails of white froth in their wakes.

With the slowing of time above the heavens, the fleet had covered thousands of leagues in the minutes the Angeli had been watching. Their faces were serene and beautiful and emotionless, even as the fleet approached the island at the center of Mysterion's ocean.

Only Azrel appeared at all bothered at the sight of the attack. She fluttered ahead of the rest of the host, then drifted behind. She stared into the faces of her companions with a mute urgency. And while she maintained the customary silence of the Angeli, it was an obvious and painful effort for her to do so.

At last, she could no longer contain herself. "Well?" she said. "What is your word? Is it the will of Wind?"

The others glanced at her with faint disapproval. They knew she was rude, but her outbursts were still disturbing.

Uhrizel spoke for them all, with a touch of sternness. "That is not certain yet." He turned his attention back below.

"But it's obvious," Azrel persisted. "The Elder is captive, and he needs our intervention. What is there to think about?"

Uhrizel sighed. "None of us acts alone. And none of us acts until we all confirm the voice of the Wind. You know that, and yet in the past you have intervened with unseemly haste, with consensus barely voiced . . ."

"Because it was clear what the Wind wanted," Azrel said.

"Nevertheless," Uhrizel said, "you will wait until we have all agreed."

Azrel sulked. The rest of the Angeli returned to their silent surveillance. The sun had set over Mysterion's ocean. A silver coat of moonlight covered the surface. The fleet had slowed to a crawl. Without solar power, the hover-ships now had to rely on the wind alone, their flat-bottomed hulls ungainly in the waves. The Angeli kept up their vigil, and moments later, the sun ascended, the fleet powering back to life, driving on to the east. Within two days—a few minutes from now, in the Angeli's frame of reference—the Mezoramians would reach the island and launch their attack.

Azrel drifted over beside Shantiel, and spoke into her mind, *You know I'm right. Why didn't you speak up?*

Shantiel didn't look at her. *We have to work together, Azrel. We can't put ourselves at odds with others. From the beginning, the Wind told us to intervene only when called. Our consensus safeguards us—"*

I know the doctrine, Azrel snapped. *But there's such a thing as common sense.*

Yes, Shantiel replied, a smiling touching her lips. *And it's called* common *for a reason.*

*Well, I wish—*Azrel said, then stopped. On Mysterion, the sun had set again. Something in the darkness held Azrel's attention.

What is it? Shantiel said, following the direction of her gaze.

"Don't you see?" Azrel said out loud, drawing irritated glances all around them.

"Yes, but . . ." Shantiel murmured, her eyes apologizing to the others. "So what?"

"They're going to force their fate," Azrel said. "Do you understand?"

Shantiel looked down, reading what she saw below. On the surface of the ocean, dark was giving way to dawn again.

"Perhaps . . ." Shantiel said. "But if so, it is out of our hands."

"What is the consensus?" Azrel said to Uhrizel. "I need to know now!"

Uhrizel looked around, angry but uncertain. "I am not . . ."

"Enough!" Azrel said. "I'm going. Shun me if you want!" And she dove like a meteor toward the surface. The host watched, the urgent fluttering of their countless wings the only sign of their consternation.

"Go with her," Uhrizel said to Shantiel. "Only you can keep her in check."

"But," Shantiel said, "do we have consensus?"

Uhrizel looked around. "Yes," he sighed. "Not that it matters now. Go, quickly, before she does something reckless."

Relieved to have permission, Shantiel plummeted down through Okean and into Mysterion in pursuit of her friend.

Chapter Sixteen

The Mezoramian hover-ships took to the waves with the reluctance of vessels far out of their natural element. The engineers who had conceived and designed them had never envisioned ocean journeys by night. At most, they had allowed for the possibility that sunset might catch the ships as they crossed the swamps to the north and south of the deserts. On those rare occasions, the solar sails might be used in the traditional manner, and the flat-bottomed hulls could navigate the shallowest of waters.

Nothing like this. The ships struggled up each wave and collapsed into the troughs, their hulls slapping hard on the surface rather than cutting through. The water resisted their progress, exploding off the rounded prows. Together, they made a few knots, almost at a standstill on the moonlit ocean.

As the cool air of the desert nights had yielded to the close damp heat of the ocean, the warriors had abandoned their quarters below and laid their sleeping mats on the open decks. They lay in rows, tossing and turning, unaccustomed to the buck and toss of the hull on waves. The mosquitoes that descended on them as soon as the sun went down only added to the misery and sleeplessness of their nights.

On the Mighty One's flagship, Sartish was also sleepless, though for different reasons. He lay flat on his back on a sleeping mat in the atrium of the master's cabin, which occupied the stern of the ship. A heavy curtain partitioned the atrium from the main deck, swaying in the wind. Around him, Tasarakt's personal attendants snored, coughed, and occasionally slapped at themselves when a mosquito bit.

Under other circumstances, Sartish would have slept soundly despite the heat, the movements of the hull, and even the mosquitoes. Aside from being used to these disturbances, the weeks before the fleet set out had exhausted him, days filled from end to end with the combat training sessions that Tasarakt had ordered for him. Instructors had drilled him morning and afternoon in the fire-bow, the spear, and the shotel, until they admitted (with some reluctance) that he stood a good chance of surviving a battle. They had tried to teach him the rudiments of military acrobatics, but in this area, Sartish had been less successful. When he dislocated his shoulder after a failed flip, Tasarakt forbade further sessions.

"You will need to remain in your place anyway," he said with a faint smile. "Just watch and do what you are told."

Between the training sessions and drills, the Mighty One had required Sartish to attend the noonday liturgies and appointed a tutor to instruct him in the basics of Mezoramian teachings concerning the pure Light, along with readings from the books of the Lord and Father and his various commentators. Every evening, he and his tutor were expected on Tasarakt's private balcony overlooking the courtyard. They listened to a steady stream of poets and musicians offer their latest compositions, while the tutor commented in a low murmur on the finer points of each performance.

When Sartish at last crawled onto his sleeping mat after midnight, his muscles screaming and his mind numb, he could not resist the weight of his eyelids. He thought he would never return to consciousness again. But a few hours later, he was staring at the ceiling as Jonah's face floated above, sad and serene. The rest of the night, he kept his eyes shut, dozing fitfully and waking exhausted for another full day.

After what felt like months to Sartish, the commanders assembled before Tasarakt and reported that all the preparations were complete. The ships had been serviced and stocked with dried meat and fruit and casks of fresh water. The regiments had mustered at the outer walls, awaiting orders to board, and reserve warriors had been called up to protect the city in their absence. The star navigators had scoured the archives, searching the lowest levels to find crumbling copies of the ancient charts, from which they had plotted a course to where the Lord and Father and his clan had begun their journey, at the time of the Battle. The foreigner could direct them to his island from there.

The Council went through the motions of deliberating, and then voted unanimously to give the launch order. The following morning, as the sun rose furnace-red, three hundred hover-ships sped away in arrowhead formation while the crowds lined the top of the walls, roaring and waving long white banners. At the stern rail, Sartish watched the Floating City sink below the dunes. When the last of the spires vanished, he exhaled a long breath. The irresistible weight of exhaustion crashed in on him.

But any hope of respite was short-lived. One of the servants hurried over. Tasarakt had ordered him to attend his cabin.

"There you are," Tasarakt waved him in. "Sit down. I need to ensure that your tutor has correctly instructed you . . ."

From that day and every day until just last evening, Tasarakt had grilled him on his knowledge of Mezoramian culture, correcting his slightest mistakes as the courtiers chuckled and shook their heads. In the brief breaks between the sessions, Sartish leaned against the rail, staring at the water but not seeing it. The humiliating bombardment of the Mighty One's interrogations had left him numb with misery.

He thought about Jonah during those moments, and during the nights, when sleep continued to elude him.

Should I have followed him? He asked himself yet again. Another voice, his own but fiercer, answered, *Don't be a fool! You were making the correct choice, and now that it's hard, you want to run back home?*

He thought about the Djinn, that horned skeletal head grinning up at him from the surface of the drinking pool. What had he said? *"The time is coming when the Djinn will break the bonds of the curse the Lamp placed on us . . . We will bring order to this world . . . We will need allies, rulers among their races, to ensure that peace is maintained, to be a voice for those in their care. You can be one of those rulers . . ."*

What if the demon was right? What if they *did* escape? Would Jonah lead a fight against them? Sartish couldn't imagine it. No, the Elder was weak, and there would be no place for the weak if the Djinn came back.

And yet even now, Jonah's face continued to float before his eyes, filled with the sadness that Sartish could not evade.

Enough! He thought, sitting up. *I have to look him in the face, and be done with it!*

He threw aside the cotton sheet, picked his way among the sleeping bodies, and slipped out through the curtains.

The guard on duty looked around.

"I have to use the head," Sartish muttered, indicating a

nearby hatchway. The guard turned back to his watch. Sartish descended the ladder. The space below the main deck was large and open. The masts, wrapped in coils of copper wire, descended through the floor to the engines and fans below. Supporting posts and beams divided the space at regular intervals along the deck. Dried meat and bags of dried fruit hung in swaying rows along the beams, while barrels of water were lashed to the posts. The heat was a solid thing, intensified by the oil lamps along the walls. No wonder everyone had gone up to sleep on the main deck, despite the insects, Sartish thought as he hurried toward the stern.

The head and the brig were located side by side under the navigation deck, the stench of the one enhancing the punishment of the other. Combined with the heat and humidity, the air became almost unbreathable as Sartish approached. He struggled to contain his impulse to heave, taking deep slow breaths.

There was no guard on duty. Tasarakt trusted in the chains, the lock, and the open water to keep his prisoners in place. Sartish peered through the bars but could not make anyone out in the pitch blackness within. The hoarse rattle of snoring told him at least that Bas Rabyah was there. And then Jonah spoke softly.

"Good to see you." With a clink of chains, the Elder rose and stepped forward against the bars. In the lamplight, his face was smeared and his dark hair tangled. From the smell of him, he hadn't washed in days.

"How have you been?" Jonah said.

"Busy," Sartish said. *There's that look*, he thought. He clenched his fists, wanting to punch Jonah through the bars.

"I suppose they want to make sure you can represent them,"

Jonah said.

"No," Sartish replied. "I wanted to learn." It wasn't entirely true, but close enough.

Jonah nodded. They were silent, looking at one another.

"Are you pitying me?" Sartish said.

"No," Jonah said.

"Then why that look? You think I am some . . ." Sartish searched, but couldn't find the right word. "Some failure?"

"No, Sartish," Jonah said with force, gripping the bars. "I am just sad about the far paths the Wind has chosen to take."

"More abstractions!" Sartish said. "What is that supposed to mean?"

"It means that I believe one day we will be companions again. But we have to journey away from each other first."

"How will that happen?" Sartish said, with a touch of scorn in his voice. "If I am not surviving the Ordeal, you will become Tasarakt's vassal. If I *am* surviving, Tasarakt cannot afford to keep you alive. Either way, there is no journey. One of us dies, that's all. Unless you are talking about that so-called *Higher Mysterion*, in which case you can believe what you want if it is making you feel any better."

"There's another option," Jonah said.

Sartish frowned. "What is that?"

"You could free us."

Sartish's laugh was humorless, angry. "Why? So you can rally the People to your side, and turn them against me?"

"I wouldn't do that," Jonah said.

"And even if you did," Sartish continued, as if he hadn't heard, "when Tasarakt discovered that I was the betrayer, he would execute me, destroy the pirates, and take the People back to Mezoramia as slaves."

"Listen to me, Sartish."

"Either way, we lose," Sartish said. He could hear the trembling in his voice, and hated himself for it. "So again, why?"

"For the sake of our friendship," Jonah said.

Sartish laughed again and shook his head. "No."

"You should know me by now," Jonah said. "I would never do anything to put you in danger. I have no intention of competing with you to lead the People of the Wind. You should not have to face the Ordeal . . ."

"Why?" Sartish demanded. "Because you think I would not survive?"

"Because I wouldn't wish it on my worst enemy, let alone my best friend!"

Sartish was thrown off guard. *Did he mean that? Or was just trying to butter me up?*

"Then what?" he said. "You think I am just going to trust and believe that my best friend will, what, go away forever?"

"Yes," Jonah said. "I would go into exile among the Solitaries."

"And you think Tasarakt is going to believe that?" Sartish said, incredulous. "You must be simple in the head!"

"No, he won't," Jonah said calmly. "Because he will believe Bas and I are dead. In fact, he will believe you killed us."

Sartish stared at him, speechless. His thoughts whirled like leaves in a storm. The clear, bright anger he had brought down with him, which had burned with such intensity just moments before, had given way to a tumult of emotions that blended in something whose color he could not identify with any certainty.

"He will be angry, of course," Jonah said. "He may threaten you. But in the end, he will understand that you were just clearing away a rival. And then, he will have to entrust you with care of the People."

"And then?" Sartish managed.

"Then we go our separate ways, until the Wind blows us back together again."

"I . . ." Sartish shook his head, confused, trying to catch his thoughts as they spun through his mind. "I don't know . . ."

"Do you remember what Tala told us, Sartish?" Jonah said, leaning forward so his face touched the bars. "She said that everything could be conquered by stillness. I didn't believe her. I thought there was a middle way. You didn't trust me to lead the People in a fight against our enemies, and you were right. I wasn't willing to make that choice. Now I know that Tala was right. There's no middle way. It's either fight or stay still, and I want to stay still. The question is, do you trust me to do that?"

* * *

After Sartish left, Bas Rabyah, who had woken during the conversation, said, "Are you sure you want to risk this, Lord?"

Jonah sighed. "It's a bit late now, isn't it?"

"But what if they will not come in to get us?" Bas Rabyah said. "They did not even wish to *touch* the water before . . ."

"Then we forced our fate," Jonah said. "And we must accept the consequences of that."

"But need we run toward our fate?" Bas said. "I may have lived a full life, but I am not eager to die again."

Jonah reached out and gripped the old man's shoulder.

"I know," Bas Rabyah sighed. "Trust the Wind. And I do. I simply wish that trust was not such a terrifying matter."

Jonah smiled in the darkness. "That reminds me of something I said to Sartish."

* * *

The guards brought Jonah and Bas Rabyah up on deck after daybreak. The rays of the rising sun had brought the fleet of hover-ships to life. Beneath them, the hull reverberated to the roar of the fans as they drove on toward the east, leaving a trail of foam behind. Tasarakt and his entourage had assembled in front of his quarters. Sartish stood among them, his heart beating so loudly in his ears, he wondered if anyone else could hear it. As the guards hustled the Elder and Bas forward, his palms started sweating.

Tasarakt regarded the prisoners, his eyes forbidding. "Do you recall on what condition I allowed the apostate to come?"

Jonah's eyes met Tasarakt's without flinching. "Yes."

"Do you recall the consequences of your disobedience?"

Jonah said nothing.

"Yet you chose to throw his life away! You could have left him to his exile, but instead you condemned him to death!"

"My People are too precious," Jonah said. "Bas Rabyah has lived his life and died. He has made his choices freely."

"That is true, Mighty One," Bas Rabyah said, raising his head. "I urged the Elder not to hesitate on my account."

Tasarakt leaned back, impressed in spite of his anger. "If you are indeed willing to sacrifice one man for the many you rule, then perhaps I underestimated you. Perhaps you are a leader after all. In the future, I will have to select a hostage more carefully, perhaps someone younger." He addressed the guards. "Throw the old man overboard. Drowning will be a painful enough death for him."

"You have no need to throw me," Bas said. "I will go myself." Without waiting, he strode to the railing, his back very straight. As he opened the gate, there was a hum beneath deck and a plank slid from the side of the ship. Bas Rabyah started along the plank, teetering as the turbulent water rushed below.

"Wait!" Sartish said. Bas Rabyah stopped. Everyone turned to gape at him, including Tasarakt. Sartish pointed at an accusing finger at Jonah. "He incites me to commit treason, and you punish the old man? Put them both in!" He leapt at Jonah, and shoved him toward the railing. Jonah made no effort to resist, giving ground before Sartish as he stumbled backwards. The guards behind them, recovering from their surprise, sprang forward in pursuit, but Sartish was too quick. They collided with Bas Rabyah and tumbled into the turbulent waters. Sartish stopped himself just in time at the edge of the plank, arms wind-milling. Jonah and Bas had vanished beneath the foaming water.

Sartish made his way back to the main deck. Tasarakt's face was now black with fury. As they faced each other, everyone waited to see what would happen next. On the nearest ships, onlookers lined the railings.

"How dare you," Tasarakt said. "How dare you defy me!"

"What else were you expecting?" Sartish replied. "It was him or me. I chose me."

Tasarakt glowered at him.

"Besides, what difference does it make for you?" Sartish said. "Now, his people have to follow me. And I follow you."

Tasarakt glanced sideways at one of his courtiers. The man cowered under his gaze. Then the Mighty One burst into laughter, his hands fluttering in the air like birds startled into flight. "You foreigners have hidden depths of ruthlessness! Very well then. It seems you will have to do for our purposes." He looked at Sartish with dark speculation in his eyes. "And it seems you have what is necessary to do well."

"Thank you, Mightiness," Sartish said. He was thinking of Jonah and Bas, sinking under the weight of their chains.

In the excitement, no one noticed two objects—strangely fishlike—drop out of the sky and hit the water in their wake.

Chapter Seventeen

zrel hurtled toward the ocean surface of Mysterion. She burst through the dome of stars and planets, dragging eddies of astral dust in her wake. To her left, the moon was a faint outline on the western edge of the world, while opposite the flaming ball of the sun ascended skyward, trailing orange and gold.

Azrel saw none of that beauty. She watched Jonah and Bas Rabyah hit the water, and now her gaze followed their writhing bodies down through the sun-beamed depths, shoals of fish scattering before them.

The mind of an Elemental is always clear. Even when disturbed, it is transparent in its goals. So, when Elementals make a decision, they do so with a single-mindedness unknown to most human beings. Even the Djinn possess this focus, dedicating themselves to their enmity with the Wind as the other Elementals do to their service: the Blind Watchmen to their guarding, the mermaids to keeping the dead.

Azrel's mind was, as always, clear as Okean itself. Although tossed in the storm of horror at seeing Jonah about to die again, the fear of knowing she would soon be outcast, shunned among the Angeli — she knew exactly what she was going to do next. And yet, what she was going to do next was something that her kind had not done for over a thousand years, since the Wind had allowed them to choose between earth, air, water, and fire. She could not guess what would happen after she did it, whether she would even be able to return. Still, she felt as if the Wind were at her back, stronger than ever.

A voice called from above her. "Azrel!" A flood of relief and joy mingled with the tumult of Azrel's emotions. Even if Shantiel would not follow her all the way, at least a friend would be with her when it happened.

Shantiel caught up to her. "Azrel. What are you doing?"

Azrel glanced sideways. "I am going to get them."

"But . . ." Shantiel looked bewildered. "It's too late. The mermaids are already coming for them." Deep below, Azrel could make out the formation of Aqueous Elementals, drawn by the sound of the drowning, finning their way toward Jonah and Bas, whose chained bodies swayed in the deep-sea current.

"They belong to the water now," Shantiel said. "Let them go."

"No," Azrel said. "I'm going in."

Shantiel's face spasmed. "*What?* You can't!"

"Of course I can!" Azrel snapped. "Only the Djinn can't make that choice any more. The rest of us just *won't!*"

"But . . ." Shantiel stammered. "We have a place. A role . . ." She saw Azrel's look and fell silent. *Please,* she whispered into Azrel's mind. *Even if you can come back, you'll be shunned. Don't leave me alone.*

Azrel smiled, took Shantiel's hand—*Then don't leave me alone*—and they plunged on. The ruffled surface of the ocean now spread out just a few hundred feet below them, stretching limitless in every direction.

Ready? Azrel said.

We're going to change here? Shantiel said. *But it's too high still*

. . .

"Now!" Azrel shouted out loud. At once, her feathers flared with the brilliance of phosphorus, turning into liquid. Beside her, Shantiel hesitated, then ignited herself. Their molten forms coalesced into the bodies of mermaids. Azrel, now a girl of about fifteen, had the lower body of a swordfish. Shantiel had a dark round face, and her body from the shoulders down was that of a spotted Eagle ray.

They hit the water in a headfirst dive. The water checked their speed, but still they plummeted down. Azrel's tail now drove her with powerful sweeps. Shantiel's pectoral fins beat like undersea wings to keep up.

Within seconds they reached Jonah and Bas. The pair were still alive, but their struggles had turned to spasms. Death was close. Azrel and Shantiel grabbed the companions and rocketed upward. They broke the surface, and rose into the air. Suspended for a moment, their bodies dissolved into a cloud of brilliant wings that swirled like a murmuration of starlings, then gathered into the forms of Angeli. Tossing the companions, retching and coughing, onto their backs, they rose toward the heavens.

"This was your plan?" Azrel said to Jonah. "Try to commit suicide and hope I would stop you? Are you crazy, Jonah?"

"I had to learn some things," Jonah croaked.

"And?" Azrel said. "Did you learn them?"

"Yes," Jonah said, between fits of coughing.

"Good," Azrel said. "Now that you know, where to?"

"The island . . ." Jonah said. He looked across at Bas Rabyah, whose eyes had widened.

Azrel noticed. "What? What's the problem?"

"I made a promise . . ." Jonah said. "And I intend to keep it . .

.” He looked at Bas Rabyah. “But I won’t do it alone.”

“So,” Azrel said. “The island? Are we sure?”

“Yes,” Jonah said. “The island . . . Before they get there . . .”

Chapter Eighteen

I n single-file, the Brethren snaked up the dark mountain path toward the plateau. At their head, Disagree ran with Isabella, bound and slung over his shoulder, and a flaming torch held up to light the way. Hodoul and Madame Razor followed close on his heels, taking the path in strides, then the senior among the crew, driving forward, eager with bloodlust. The rest of the horde were a swirling lake of torchlight at the base of the mountain, shouting and jostling each other to be next onto the path.

The Angeli had soared overhead before descending to the mountaintop, which now glowed as if lit by a beacon of fire.

"One more hour," Madame Razor panted, "and we could have finished them. Now we have to contend with those . . . things!"

"I believe that they are committed to non-interference in human affairs," Hodoul said, also sounding winded. "But even if they should decide to lend a hand, we still have our little hostage here to negotiate with."

Disagree did not look back. From the moment that Isabella had chosen to go with him back down the mountain, his heart had tied itself into knots. It was a sensation that reminded him of the nightmare, looking down at the stone. He knew that the king would keep Isabella alive until he had the plateau. And then . . . *And then*, Disagree thought. *I pick up the rock.* He knew it was coming, a black hole toward which he was rushing. The fear of it had paralyzed his insides, even as he went through the motions with his customary impassivity, so that no one, not even Hodoul, could have guessed his feelings.

They scaled the final stretch. The light around them intensified. Finally they reached the top, and the radiance of the Angeli—floating several feet above the plateau like twin suns—drove the night away. A crowd confronted them—people of all ages, none of them armed—with Jonah at their center. Beside him stood a skinny old man whom Disagree did not recognize, and the little girl he had seen before, clinging to Jonah's leg. There was something sad about her eyes that Disagree found disturbing.

Hodoul dragged Isabella off Disagree's shoulders and hauled her forward. Behind them, a stream of Brethren spilled off the path and onto the plateau, encircling the People with swords drawn and rifles cocked.

"Forgive me," Isabella said to Jonah. Her tear-stained face was desolate.

"There's nothing to forgive," Jonah said softly. "Shantih told me."

"Yes, Bella-Bella," Shantih piped up. "I told him you did right."

Jonah glanced at Disagree. "I hope you understand what a friend you have."

Disagree did not respond.

"I cannot believe I am hearing this," Hodoul said. Although the king was smiling with incredulity, Disagree could tell from the way he held Isabella in front of him and the tension of his body that he was nervous. He darted glances at the hovering

Angeli, who looked down on them, calm and inscrutable.

"Let me see if I understand this correctly," Hodoul said to Jonah. "You abandon your people. They have no idea whether you will return. Then one day, you float down from the skies, and they flock to your side. *She*—" he gestured at Isabella—"even apologizes. These people of yours are worse than sheep!"

"Or perhaps they know how to trust," Jonah said. "But you are right. I delayed. And I am humbled by their patience."

Madame Razor laughed. "How sweet!"

"Isn't he?" Hodoul smiled back at her. "To tell you the truth, my dear, I almost envy how easily he controls them. Still," he raised his voice, so it would carry. "Give me this lot any day, proud and stubborn. And free!"

The Brethren cheered. Their eyes were eager, like hunting dogs waiting to be unleashed.

"And this is what free people do, is it?" Jonah said. "Attack innocent and unarmed men, women, and children?"

"Can you blame the shark for chasing blood?" Hodoul said.

"Not sharks," Jonah said. "Only people who act like sharks."

"You exalt human beings too highly," Hodoul said. "We are just animals, after all."

"We will have to agree to disagree on that point," Jonah said.

Hodoul raised his hands. "I suppose we will. Now . . ." He drew his dagger and pressed it against Isabella's throat. "Please ask your winged friends to return to wherever they came from, and surrender yourselves."

Every muscle in Disagree's body drove him to step forward and grab at Hodoul's hand. But he could feel Madame Razor watching, waiting for him to betray himself. If he moved now, there would be no going back.

With a vast effort, he restrained himself, keeping his face expressionless. Madame Razor's disappointment was palpable.

Jonah glanced up at the Angeli. "You may not know this, but the Angeli have never taken sides in human conflicts."

"Then why are they here?" Hodoul said.

"We're still looking at the options," Azrel replied.

Hodoul squinted up at her. "What does that mean?"

Azrel shrugged. "You just said you weren't human, so perhaps that means we can get involved after all . . ."

"Azrel!" Jonah said fiercely. He said to Hodoul, "On my word, they will not attack you. Just let Isabella go. We will leave peacefully, and you can have the island." Around him, the People uttered a collective gasp. A chorus of protest rose up. Hodoul watched them with amusement. Shantih tugged at Jonah.

"But this is the Elder's Island," she cried. "He gave it to us!"

"No, Shantih," Jonah took her hand and turned to face the People. "When the Elder returned to the Wind, he appointed me to care for you. Not for a place, a piece of land—*you*, his People. I made a promise that I would go into exile, and I am going. But I won't go alone. I want you all to come with me."

The anxious commotion died away. In the silence, a gust of wind breathed off the dim expanse beyond the dome of light.

Jonah turned back to Hodoul. "Let her go. You can have what you want."

"What I want," Hodoul said, pressing the blade against Isabella's throat, "is for you to tell those creatures to go away."

The knots around Disagree's heart tightened. He didn't know how much longer he could maintain his composure.

"I chose this, Jonah," Isabella said. "I'll live with what comes."

"How noble!" Hodoul said. "Now please shut up, my dear Isabella, or I will open up your windpipe and silence you myself."

Bas Rabyah leaned over to Jonah. "Lord," he whispered. "My bow. I can—"

Jonah put a hand on the old man's shoulder. "No, Bas," he murmured. "Wait, please." He addressed Hodoul. "Be reasonable. I won't throw my People to your sharks and you won't risk losing an attack against the Angeli. However, *we* can wait for as long as we need to, while *you* are running out of time."

Hodoul frowned. "What are you talking about?"

"After the Falls, I traveled to the west to look for some help, people who could fight for us. I didn't find what I was looking for, but still, help is coming. By my estimation, they will be here just after daybreak."

"Who are *they*?" Hodoul said. Disagree was sure no one else could hear the anxiety behind the king's contempt.

Jonah indicated the forest behind him. "Come and see."

Hodoul's cold eyes followed Jonah's gesture. "Is this some kind of trick?"

Jonah shook his head. "Not at all. Do you recall the pool beside the Djinn's Tree?"

"What about it?" Hodoul said.

"They have one," Jonah said. "But we have more than anyone can count. And we can see anywhere in Mysterion. We can even see into the world of the Lethes. When we leave, the Seeing Pools will be yours. You will be able to see your enemies, whatever they happen to be doing at this moment."

Jonah paused. In the silence that followed, he did not break eye contact with Hodoul. Watching them, Disagree knew that the king's mind was working through all the angles, though his face betrayed nothing.

"Very well," Hodoul said finally. "I will humor you. You and I and this pathetic girl will go and see. And when we return, we will complete our business once and for all." He turned to Madame Razor. "My dear?"

She waved. "Enough talking. Go. But hurry. The sharks are hungry!" Thick laughter rippled among the Brethren.

The crowd parted before Jonah as he led the way toward the forest. Hodoul followed, driving Isabella before him. They disappeared into the trees. As the minutes dragged by, the Brethren grew restless. They gathered in sullen knots, and though Disagree could not make out the exact content of their words, he knew that the truce would not last much longer. Someone was going to try and take a shot.

Madame Razor looked around at them. "Enough!" she shouted. "Patience!" She smiled up at Azrel. "I can't hold them back much longer. And to tell you the truth, dearie," she put her hand to the side of her mouth in a gesture of mock confidence, "I don't want to. The king may think you're some kind of threat to us, but I say we should see just how serious you are, and let the dice fall where they may!"

"We are creatures of air who just dived to the bottom of the sea to raise the Elder from the dead," Azrel replied. "Do you really think I'm going to let you degenerates lay a hand on any one of these people?"

Madame Razor's eyes glittered. Her smile tightened. "You can't stop every shot."

"Try us," Azrel said.

By now, the Brethren had lost interest in their mutinous conclaves. In the silence, all eyes were fixed on them.

She is good, Disagree thought. *Almost as good as him.*

"Hear that, brothers and sisters?" Madame Razor said, looking around. "The creatures want us to try them. Shall we?" She raised her hand. The Brethren cheered and began to press forward. The People of Wind drew together, holding one another. Their plaintive voices rose up, like a colony of sea-birds.

"The king says to wait," Disagree said to Madame Razor.

"He's not the only one wearing pants," Madame Razor snapped, "and you will do what you're told. Finish them!"

Rifle-fire erupted around the circle, but the Angeli had already broken into flight. They encircled the People, their forms dissolving into a ring of light against which the volley bounced, killing several attackers.

"Enough!" Hodoul roared. The king strode out of the forest, dragging Isabella by her chains. Behind him, Jonah followed at a slower pace, almost sauntering. Disagree thought, *he looks like he has won.*

The Angeli continued their protective circling, concealing the People of the Wind behind a barrier of light. Hodoul paid them no attention. "Everyone down to the ships. Weigh anchor and link the blockade!"

The Brethren froze, staring at him. Madame Razor put her hands on her hips. "What is this now? What's happening?"

"We will be under attack by tomorrow," Hodoul said. "We need to be ready."

Madame Razor examined his face, then swung around. "You heard the king. Board ship and man the linking chains!"

As the Brethren shoved to make their way onto the path, Hodoul turned to Disagree. "Take the girl and make sure she is secure in the brig, out of harm's way. We will need her for future negotiations."

As Disagree lifted Isabella onto his shoulder, glimpsing the quiet resignation in her eyes, a sudden insight came to him: the king would never let her go. He might not kill her, but she would always be in chains. And she was just the first. After the Brethren had taken this island, there would be other hostages taken from every conquered place, all kept in chains to ensure the loyalty of their people.

He saw the desolation of it like a grey featureless landscape crowded with faceless, hopeless men and women. And in that place, who would he be? Would he be the one who guarded those lost souls? And all for the hope that somehow, Hodoul would one day be inspired to have compassion at last?

"We will return, boy," Hodoul said to Jonah. "For now, watch how the Brethren deal with those who come against them!"

"The Wind is turning," Jonah said softly. "Can you feel It?"

For a brief instant, naked hatred blazed in Hodoul's face. Then it vanished, the familiar cold exterior returning. He turned to Madame Razor. "Well, my dear. Shall we put our new partnership to the test?"

"About time," she declared. "Let's go!"

* * *

As the rays of the rising sun reached up from the eastern sky behind them, the People of the Wind gathered to watch the Brethren fleet link up. Fore and aft guns puffed white smoke, the explosions carrying to the plateau seconds later. Lines, thin as a thread from this distance, arced out to the adjacent ships, followed by chains that ant-sized crew members pulled on board and secured bow and stern. By the time the sun rose above the trees, the ships were chained together, a floating barrier around the island.

Jonah paced along the edge of the plateau, his eyes fixed on *La Justice* below, trying—and failing—to identify Isabella among the tiny figures that scurried about the deck. Nearby, Shantih followed his movements with dark eyes. Bas Rabyah was nowhere to be seen, having disappeared into the forest before dawn. The Angeli had returned to their positions, fluttering in slow circles above the plateau.

Even as light spilled over the ocean, darkness crowded every corner of Jonah's mind. He had hoped to lead the People into exile, carrying the Lamp to protect them from their enemies until the Higher Mysterion. All of that had disintegrated last night, the moment Azrel had floated down to the plateau and Shantih had raced forward with tears streaming down her cheeks to throw herself into his arms.

The Lamp was gone. Pierre was gone with it. Hodoul had Isabella, and the chances that the pirate king would let her go were non-existent. He would almost certainly use her to force them to do . . . who knew what?

Jonah pressed his fingers into his eyes. *What now? Just stand here and watch? And it doesn't even matter who wins . . .*

A hand gripped his shoulder. Jonah turned to face Bas Rabyah. In one hand the old man held a recurved bow. It was made of several metals braided together—silver, gold, copper, and others that Jonah could not identify. The string was also woven from metal threads. At the nocking point, it attached to a strange assembly, a copper coil around a cylinder extending from a point just above the grip.

"The fire bow I won at contest," Bas Rabyah said, as if guessing Jonah's thoughts. "The one I used to defend the Elder during the years of his exile. After he liberated Mysterion, I buried it in the forest beside one of the Seeing Pools, the one that looks into Mezoramia. It took me some time to find it in the dark."

"Why did you unbury it?" Jonah asked.

Bas Rabyah's eyes were steady. "Because it is time to use it again, my Lord."

Jonah looked at him, then closed his eyes. The darkness inside him was a storm shot through with beams of light.

After everything, he thought. *We have to fight.*

"Yes," he said. "It is time to use it."

Shantih ran over and took his hand. He looked down at her.

"Are you going to bring Bella-Bella back?" she said.

"Yes, Shantih *petit,*" Jonah replied.

"Good," Shantih said softly.

Jonah nodded and looked up at Azrel and Shantiel.

"I know, I know," Azrel said. "You want us to take you down there. Better hurry and get on, then. They're here."

Jonah looked around. In the morning light, the sails of the Mezoramian fleet glittered on the horizon from end to end.

Chapter Nineteen

Sartish watched the Elder's island rise above the horizon. Nearby, Tasarakt presided over the fleet from a bench raised on a platform. At his right shoulder stood the Admiral—a gaunt old man with coal-black skin and shoulder-length woolly white hair—issuing commands in sign language that the captains to the ships port and starboard picked up and repeated, relaying the message from ship to ship down the formation. On the main deck, the warriors formed into three rows amidships. They held their fire bows at the ready, with shotels sheathed at their backs, ready to draw the moment they boarded.

Sartish was not paying attention. The shouted orders of the officers, the roar of the fans beneath the deck, the explosions of white foam churned up as the ship skimmed the waves—all of it came to him from a distance, as if he had gone into a soundproof room and closed the door. Only the island filled his vision, its peak reaching up almost until it touched the rising sun, pushing everything else to the edges.

The knot in the pit of his stomach had persisted since the previous day. Moments after the armada had powered away from where Jonah and Bas had drowned, Sartish had watched the Angeli fall and rise again, like slow lightning. The Mezoramians had interpreted the sight as a heavenly sign of impending victory against the Degenerates. Sartish had known better, and for the first time, allowed himself to hope.

The sight had flipped his hope into a darker emotion, the knot in his gut tying itself for the first time. If the Angeli *had* rescued Jonah and Bas, would Jonah keep his word and go quietly into exile with the Solitaries? Or would he be waiting at the top of the mountain when the Mezoramians arrived, with the People at his back? If he was, it would all come down to the Ordeal of Windfire . . . Sweat broke out on Sartish's palms. The thought of reaching out, taking hold of that Lamp himself . . .

And if he survived, what was to guarantee that Tasarakt wouldn't choose Jonah to lead the People of the Wind anyway, taking a hostage to ensure his obedience? For Sartish to have to submit to Jonah after all this was . . . humiliating. On the other hand, if Tasarakt chose him, what would happen to Jonah? He was too much of threat to be kept alive, and Tasarakt would not risk sending him into exile.

Maybe it was too late, his other voice said. *Maybe they are with the Sleepers now. That would be best, would it not?*

Tasarakt's voice cut into his thoughts. "Perhaps you should take shelter below deck, with the rest of my entourage."

Sartish turned, almost relieved to escape from his thoughts. Tasarakt was regarding him with an amused smile.

"After all," the Mighty One continued, "I would not want my figurehead to be damaged or broken in the battle."

The Admiral chuckled. Even the helmsman grinned.

Sartish met and held Tasarakt's eyes. "With your blessing, Mightiness, I will remain at your side in the battle. In addition, I would be honored to receive a fire bow, that I might defend you against the Degenerates."

Tasarakt laughed, his hands breaking into flight. "Well

done!" he cried. "You are almost one of us. Yes, you have my blessing. You may take your place with the guard that will shield me during the battle."

Half an hour later, Sartish clambered back onto the navigation deck wearing a white-and-gold uniform, with a round shield bound to his chest and a fire-bow and shotel strapped to his back. The Elder's island was close enough now to take up the whole horizon. Sartish could make out the blockade of Brethren ships strung out at regular intervals ahead of them, with chains linking them fore and aft.

They were prepared for us, he thought. *Someone told them we were coming . . .* The knot in his stomach twisted tighter.

The Mighty One surveyed the scene through an ornate copper telescope resting on a tripod. His bodyguards had formed a line around the platform. Tasarakt glanced up as Sartish appeared, and gestured. "Take your place." Feeling self-conscious, Sartish found a gap in the line and stood to attention.

He heard Tasarakt address the Admiral. "Begin."

There was a silence as the Admiral conveyed his orders. From the corner of his eye, Sartish could see the captain on the ship to port, repeating the hand gestures precisely as he had received them. Within moments, they would begin the bull's horns maneuver to encircle the island and attack the Brethren on all fronts.

The blockade was close enough now that Sartish could identify each of the ships. *La Justice* lay ahead, broadside and slightly to starboard. Further along the line, Madame Razor's sleek schooner, *The Black Cat*, tossed against the restraint of the chains. Cannons bristled from the gaping portholes of every vessel. In the empty spars, snipers nestled, waiting to pick off the enemy from above, while the rest of the Brethren lined the railings, waving rifles in the air, their battle cries not quite lost in the roar of the fans and the churning of the sea into white water around them.

Sartish pointed at *La Justice*. "Mightiness!" he called. "The pirate king's ship!"

There was a brief pause of surprise behind him. Then Tasarakt said, "Adjust course. If he falls, the rest will follow him!"

At once, the flagship angled to starboard to bring them onto a direct heading toward *La Justice*. The ships on either side matched the movement to maintain the arrowhead formation.

"Prepare for full stop and broadside!" the Admiral told the helmsman.

"Yes, Lord!" the helmsman said.

"Archers to the ready!" the Admiral shouted down to the main deck. The captains repeated the order, and the rows of warriors stepped forward, raised, drew their fire-bows, pointing them skyward.

On *La Justice*, Hodoul raised his hand. When that hand dropped, the Brethren would also unleash their firepower.

"On my mark!" the Admiral said.

A bright movement high in the air caught Sartish's attention. The others were too preoccupied to notice it, but for him, the flickering was familiar. He raised his eyes. His heartbeat slowed. Above the island, two lights had detached themselves from the sun, circling overhead like birds.

"It's them," Sartish said, but for some reason, he kept his voice to a murmur, and no one heard him. "Jonah is alive!"

"Mark!" the Admiral shouted. "Come broadside, and fire at will!"

Chapter Twenty

Perched on Azrel's back high above, Jonah watched the Mezoramians' arrowhead formation divide, curving outward from the center to encircle the blockade and the island. As the Mezoramian vessels came broadside, they erupted a burning shower of blue fire-arrows onto the Brethren ships. At the same time, the Brethren hurled spinning, smoky-orange cannonballs across the water, along with volleys of rifle shot from the railings and the spars where the snipers were nested. The explosions reached Jonah a moment later, and from then on, the air resounded with the bombardment.

As they circled the perimeter, Jonah saw that several of the Mezoramian vessels had taken hits and collapsed on the water, tilted over and sinking, their sides torn by the fiery cannonballs. The Brethren ships seemed unscathed by comparison, their metallic hulls smoking from the volleys of fire-arrows but not yet aflame. Still, they had taken heavy human casualties, bodies scattered across the decks.

"Perhaps they will destroy each other," Bas Rabyah commented, perched on Shantiel's back a few feet away.

"We can only hope," Azrel said.

"Azrel!" Shantiel said, with a touch of shock in her voice.

"Sorry," Azrel said. "I wasn't supposed to say that—out loud, anyway . . . Are you ready?" she asked Jonah.

"Not yet," Jonah said. "When they get to hand-to-hand fighting, they'll be distracted enough to give us a chance."

"How will you find her?" Azrel said.

"He must have put her in the brig," Jonah said, recalling the stories of old ships that he had read when he was young, when he dreamed of learning how to sail. "That's on the lowest deck, probably in the stern."

"And if she's not there?" Azrel said. "You could be searching for a while . . ."

Jonah shrugged. "Until I find her. I'm not leaving without her."

"Look." Bas Rabyah pointed. "They are rolling out the springboards."

The barrage of fire-arrows had eased from a deluge to a steady rain. Only the warriors at the back of the Mezoramian ranks continued to fire as the first rows of warriors raced forward, using the springboards that now extended from the sides to somersault themselves high into the air, flipping and landing on the main decks behind the enemy's main line. As soon as their feet touched, the warriors drew their shotels and attacked. Taken by surprise, the Brethren turned to defend themselves. The cannons fell silent as the gunners came up from below to join the battle, which now devolved into a mass of humanity struggling on every available space. Now the sounds rose up: the clashing ring of blade on blade, the incoherent wave of shouts and screams, all punctuated by the *crack* of snipers' rifles and the flash of fire-arrows as the remaining Mezoramian archers turned their sights to pick off the men in the rigging. Their bodies dropped at regular intervals to the decks below.

Having circled the island, the Angeli now hovered over *La*

Justice, where Hodoul was engaged with three Mezoramian warriors on the poop deck. Even from up here, the pirate king's skill was evident as he held off his attackers with a single cutlass that he easily switched from hand to hand. Beside him, his servant Disagree wielded an axe in each hand, beating back the waves of warriors who came at him.

"*Now* can we get down there?" Azrel said.

"Yes," Jonah said. "But only me. Shantiel and Bas won't land."

Bas Rabyah's eyes widened. "You agreed it was time to use the bow!"

"Yes," Jonah said. "You can use it to cover me. Anyone who comes for me, you take them down. Understand?"

The agony played on Bas's face for a moment. "As my Lord commands," he said at last. "No one will approach."

"Good," Jonah said. "Let's go!"

Abruptly, Azrel plummeted into a nosedive, forcing Jonah to cling to her with all his strength. *La Justice* rushed up toward them with frightening speed. As Jonah had predicted, none of the combatants looked up, focused on fending off each other's blows, even as the light of Azrel's body swelled from above. Only at the last moment did Hodoul look up, disbelief in his face, just as Azrel came to a full stop just above the deck. Crushed against her by the speed of her slowdown, Jonah slipped off and raced for the stern. "Be ready!" he shouted back at Azrel, as she rose back into the air.

As Jonah worked his way toward the stern, dodging between the dueling opponents, ducking to keep clear of their blades, he heard Hodoul shouting, but he couldn't make out the words. Then, as he approached the low door that led under the poop deck, a burly woman with a misshapen nose and broad, tattooed arms blocked his way, brandishing a scimitar in one hand and a dagger in the other.

"Where do you think you're going, luvvie?" she cried, grinning. Her face and clothes were speckled with blood.

Jonah started to answer, but before he could do so, something flashed. A burnt spot appeared in the center of the pirate's chest. Her eyes bulged, and she toppled sideways. Jonah glanced up at the bright flickering shape that was Shantiel. He couldn't make Bas Rabyah behind her brilliance, but he was there—no doubt about it. Jonah threw a quick wave, jerked the door open, and disappeared inside.

* * *

Disagree saw the bright, winged creature rocketing down toward the deck, and thought, *he is coming to get her!* He felt his heart quicken, and the dark weight over his mind lifting, but even so, he did not allow the emotion to betray itself on his face or distract him from the demands of the moment. He continued to dodge and spin, laying about him with the axe, cutting down enemy warriors as they leapt at him.

As Jonah leapt off the creature's back and ran toward the stern, the king shouted across at him. "Disagree, are you blind? Get down there! Don't let him get to her, do you hear? Kill both of them if you have to!"

Disagree looked over at Hodoul, and nodded. Fighting his way to the ladder, he neither lingered nor rushed, trying to give Jonah the time he needed without rousing the king's suspicions. When he was sure Jonah had made it through, he leapt down onto the deck and followed him below. Hodoul watched him go, frowning. As he held back his opponents with a practiced series of thrusts and cuts and parries, he edged his way toward the ladder.

* * *

From the navigation deck of the flagship, Sartish loosed arrow after arrow in quick succession, hitting more than he missed.

"For an earthworm, you are not too bad," the archer beside him said, without breaking his rhythm of pull-and-release.

"Perhaps I am not an earthworm, after all," Sartish replied, as one of his arrows found the heart of another sniper, dropping him soundlessly out of the rigging. "Perhaps I am a snake that is spitting out fire-arrows."

The man laughed. "Whatever you wish. Just do not bite your master's hand, if you want to keep your head."

Sartish did not respond. He turned his aim on the poop deck again. From the start of the attack he had tried to get a bead on Hodoul, but the pirate king's luck had been uncanny and every shot had gone wide, sometimes by less than a handbreadth. Once the warriors had landed on board, Sartish could no longer make Hodoul out among the warriors who surrounded him.

In the distraction of the battle, he had almost forgotten the Angeli. Then, like a flash of slow lightning, Azrel dropped out of the sky. The Mezoramian archers, despite their discipline, stopped firing, taken aback.

"It is one of those flying creatures that brought us the foreigners!" the Admiral cried.

"And *him*!" Tasarakt's voice was hoarse. "How did he . . ."

With a bittersweet flood of relief and fear, Sartish watched Jonah slip off Azrel's back and run into the crowd, ducking and sidestepping the knots of Brethren and warriors as he made his way toward the stern. As first Disagree and then Hodoul followed him below, Sartish felt the muscles tensing up inside him again.

His other voice spoke up, irritated, insistent. *What do you care? Let them finish it!*

"No," Sartish said. He dropped the bow and broke into a run, heedless of the indignant shouts of the Admiral and Tasarakt behind him. Reaching the edge of the navigation deck, he ignored the ladder, took a leap, and landed on his feet, sprinting toward the nearest springboard.

Every time he had tried the somersault during his training sessions in Mezoramia, he had failed to make the landing.

Let us hope this time is different, he thought.

* * *

Jonah paused to get used to the darkness, then hurried forward. The dining room and the cabin boy's nook were both deserted. Glancing over his shoulder to make sure that no one had followed him, he ran to the far end of the hallway and pushed open the door to the master's cabin. Empty. Turning away, he noticed a hatch in the floor. He yanked it open and clambered below. It was even darker down here, and he groped his way forward toward a line of light ahead until his hand bumped on a door.

Jonah took a deep breath. How would he deal with the guard? Perhaps Isabella was alone in there, but somehow Jonah doubted it. He suspected that she was valuable to Hodoul, even more than as a bargaining tool. The pirate king would protect her, if only to ensure that he alone would be the one to cut her throat.

Maybe I can surprise him . . . Jonah thought. He listened again for sounds of pursuit, someone coming down the ladder. Nothing. He took another deep breath, grasped the handle, rested his shoulder against the door, and shoved. The door flew open and Jonah rushed in. The brig was lit with a single flickering oil lamp, the cage occupying the right side of the cabin. The guard lay slumped against the bars, eyes staring, while Isabella squatted beside him, rummaging through his clothing. She leapt to her feet as Jonah entered, her arm coiling back to hurl the dagger that she clutched.

She gaped at him. "Jonah! How did you . . .?"

Jonah grinned. "I have the right friends. And you?" He gestured at the dead man. "Seems like you don't need rescuing."

"Almost," Isabella said. "Except, I can't find the key."

Jonah searched the man, feeling for the metal bulk of the cage key. Finally, he shook his head "He must not have it."

"No," Disagree said from the doorway. "I have it." He held up the key on a brass ring.

Jonah drew the sword from the dead guard's belt, and stepped back.

Isabella reached out. "No, Jonah, he won't hurt us!"

"I know he survived the Ordeal," Jonah said, pointing the sword. "But he turned back. He went back to Hodoul . . ."

"Yes," Isabella said, her eyes fixed on Disagree. "That's what the Wind called him to do, because no one else will."

Disagree said nothing.

"How do we know he won't betray us?" Jonah said.

"How do we know *anything* the Wind wants?" Isabella said. "Besides, we don't have much choice at this point. No offense, but you don't stand a chance against Dis. He'll disarm you with his bare hands."

Disagree glanced at Jonah. "That's true." He raised the axe in his other hand. "And I have this, so you have no hope."

Jonah sighed. "I know. I was never the fighting type anyway."

He dropped the blade, feeling relieved.

Disagree stepped forward, unlocked the cage. Isabella hugged him fiercely.

"I knew it," she said. "I knew you would come back to us!"

* * *

Disagree received Isabella's embrace with an absolute calm. Then, with a slow movement, he disengaged himself from her.

"Come," he said. "We go up now. We end this."

He led them up the ladder, Isabella and Jonah following behind. When his head rose above the hatchway, he paused. Hodoul stood at the end of the hallway, his bushy head lit up, and his face in shadow.

Here it is, Disagree thought.

"What is it, Dis?" Isabella called from below.

Disagree said nothing. He kept climbing and rose to his feet, facing the king. Behind him, Isabella and Jonah reached the top, each freezing at the sight of the king, then clambering up to stand at Disagree's back.

For once, Disagree was the first to break the silence. "You make me choose," he said to Hodoul. "So, I must choose."

"I should have let you hang," Hodoul said. "Put you out of your misery."

"Damn you," Isabella said, her voice cold with fury. "You bastard!"

Before Disagree could stop her, she slipped past under his arm and ran at the king, her dagger held before her.

"Stop, Bella!" Disagree shouted, thinking, *Not her too . . .*

But Isabella was lost in her fighting madness. She closed the gap between herself and Hodoul, snaking low, cutting for his legs. With a speed she could hardly believe, the king met her blade with his own, sweeping it aside, then slapped her to the ground with his free hand. Stunned, Isabella hurled the dagger. Her aim was off, and it flew wide, burying itself in the corner of the doorframe. Hodoul strode forward and kicked her back, placing his foot on her chest. Isabella cried out.

"Natalie is right," Hodoul said. "I have wasted my energy long enough on you, and you are more trouble than anyone is worth. It is time to move on!" He raised the cutlass and thrust it down, aiming for her heart.

Disagree exploded into movement, faster than he had ever done in his life. As Hodoul put his weight into his killing stroke, he leaped over Isabella, colliding with the king, driving him backwards onto the deck.

As Hodoul struggled to get out from underneath Disagree's weight, Isabella realized that something was wrong. She scrambled forward, grabbed his shoulder, and pulled with all her strength. It took both her efforts and Hodoul's before his body rolled aside.

The king's cutlass had entered his chest just beneath the rib cage, halfway to the hilt. A sheet of blood coated his skin and soaked Hodoul's white shirt a deep crimson, a puddle spreading around them on the deck.

Isabella screamed. Jonah ran forward, fell to his knees, and held her as she clung to him with desperation. Her screams overflowed, echoing in the confines of the hallways. Hodoul came to his feet, staring down at Disagree. For once, he looked confused, frowning as if trying to understand.

His eyes flickered over to Isabella. "This was your fault," he whispered. His voice rose as his face worked in rage. "You turned him against me!" He grabbed the hilt of the cutlass with two hands, dragged it free of Disagree's chest. "*He* should have been the one, not you or anyone else!" He swung back.

There was a flash of blue-white light. A hole appeared in Hodoul's chest, blackened at the edges where his shirt smoldered. Hodoul frowned, looked down at the hole. He looked around. Behind him, just outside the doorway, Sartish stood with the fire-bow raised, satisfaction etched on his face.

Hodoul pointed at him. "You! Traitor . . . You'll hang for desertion . . ." Then he collapsed sideways on top of Disagree.

Ignoring Jonah and Isabella, Sartish slung the bow and dragged Hodoul's body out onto the open deck. "The king is dead!" he shouted. "The king is dead!" The remaining crew of *La Justice*, decimated by the constant rain of fire-arrows and the deadly acrobatics of the Mezoramian warriors, had backed up against the mainmast to take their last stand. The sight of Hodoul spread-eagled on his back, staring up with the blankness of death, took the last of their heart. They dropped their weapons and fell to their knees, pleading for quarter. On *The Black Cat*, Madame Razor jammed her rapier into the deck, collapsed and raised her hands, her faced twisted with grief and rage. Her crew followed suit. After that, the surrender spread like a contagion around the perimeter. On ship after ship, the Brethren knelt, allowing the Mezoramians to bind them with chains.

Sartish turned back to Jonah and Isabella. He held his bow again, ready to fire.

"Stand up," he said.

They stood, with Jonah supporting Isabella, who still sobbed uncontrollably.

"You were lying to me," Sartish said.

"No," Jonah said. "I will go. I just won't go alone."

Sartish drew the bow and aimed, his eyes implacable. "I

should finish you. It would be easier for me, and everyone."

"Yes," Jonah said. "Friendship does tend to be inconvenient."

"You are not my friend!" Sartish shouted.

"Maybe not," Jonah said. "But you are mine. And as your friend, I'm asking you to put the bow down. Please."

Sartish held his position, the bow drawn and taut. Above, the sun reached its zenith. As the sweat beaded on Sartish's forehead, he glanced up, stared for a long moment, then turned his eyes back to Jonah.

"Come out here, where everyone can see me do it."

"Sartish, listen," Jonah said. "Bas Rabyah—"

"Come out here now!"

Jonah led Isabella forward through the doorway. "Bas!" he called upward. "Don't shoot!"

Sartish frowned. "What are you saying?" He searched the sky, but it was empty.

"Don't shoot!" Jonah repeated. They stepped on the open deck.

A bolt of light shot out of the sun, where the Angeli had concealed themselves. Azrel grabbed Jonah and Isabella, and hurtled back into the sky. A moment later, Shantiel and Bas Rabyah flew up beside them, and together they rose toward the peak of the island. Below, Sartish followed their trajectory and loosed a series of fire-arrows, all of which stopped short several feet below the Angeli.

Sartish lowered his bow. The battle for Elder's island was over, but grief and anger continued to war in his face.

Chapter Twenty-One

Tasarakt led the way up the path toward the plateau. The sun was falling toward the western horizon in a blaze of red-tinged clouds. The Mighty One moved with surprising speed, his steps quick and light. He did not pause for rest or to catch his breath. Part way up, the Admiral had winded himself, begging Tasarakt's forgiveness and asking his leave to turn back, as he was not the young man he used to be.

"Go," Tasarakt said. "The guards and I should be able to deal with a helpless rabble and their spineless leader."

Sartish kept pace with him all the way, but even he soon found himself panting, wiping sweat running into his eyes.

As they approached the top, Jonah, Isabella, and Bas Rabyah appeared. Bas had his bow drawn, aiming down at Tasarakt. Behind Sartish, the guards drew their own bows, ready to loose a volley in response.

"Hold!" Tasarakt shouted. "Hold!" And then, to Bas Rabyah, "What kind of defense is this? Where is your weapon of fire?"

"It was taken in my absence," Jonah said. "Thrown into the sea."

Tasarakt burst into laughter. "And you think you can resist us with an old man and his bow? How pathetic you are!"

"We may not be able to resist your army, Mightiness," Bas

Rabyah replied. "But *you* would never see the victory."

Jonah placed his hand on Bas Rabyah's shoulder. "We have no interest in killing. We have nothing for you except this island, and you are welcome to have it. All I ask is that those of my People who want to would be allowed to follow me into exile. And your word that you will allow us to leave in peace."

Tasarakt's voice was scornful. "Let you go, so that you can return and incite rebellion?"

Jonah raised his hands. "I value their freedom. If they choose to stay, and you treat them well, why would they rebel?"

Tasarakt inclined his head, acknowledging the point. He glanced over his shoulder at Sartish. "And how do I know that those who remain will accept him as their leader? There is no way for him to prove his worthiness."

"I will assure them," Jonah said. "In the end, they know his heart is with them. They can stay with him, or go with me, as the Wind blows them. There will be no betrayal in staying, nor any more merit in leaving."

The words dislodged something inside Sartish. The anger that had resisted the waves of sadness in him collapsed like a wall of sand. The tears welled up, filled his eyes. Quickly, he wiped them away, but Tasarakt had turned away, immersed in thought, considering the proposal. "Very well," he said at last. "Go, you and those who wish to follow you. You have until sundown to go, and never return."

"One more request," Jonah said.

"You dare to push me further?" Tasarakt said, incredulous.

"No," Jonah said. "It's just one of my People cannot choose to follow me, though I know he would if he were able." He glanced sideways at Isabella, who wiped at her eyes. "He was killed during the battle. I ask your Mightiness's permission to take him, so that we can honor his body in our own way."

"Fine, fine!" Tasarakt snapped. "Take him. Remember, you have until sunset!"

* * *

On the eastern side of the island, the sun had long ago fallen behind the mountains, throwing beams of red and gold toward the sky. On the beach, several small fishing boats lay on the sand at the breaker-line. Around each boat a handful of men and women, most of them young, arranged and secured what few belongings they had been able to carry down from the plateau. While the adults worked, their children scurried back and forth from the forest, carrying armfuls of fallen coconuts, mangos, and bananas to add to the stores. Others carried gourds brimming with water from a nearby stream.

Nearby, another crowd watched in silence—Sartish and the People who had chosen to remain. It was by far the larger of the two groups—the older ones, the infirm, those who were simply afraid of what might lie beyond the horizon. The sight saddened Jonah, but he could not linger on it. The loading was complete. His People had boarded, the strongest men shoving the boats afloat and hauling at the oars to get them beyond the breakers. There they paused, waiting for Jonah's boat, which was still beached.

Shantih sat in the bow, knees pulled up to her chin. Isabella, her face pale, sat amidships beside Disagree's body, which was wrapped in the customary white cloth. In the shallows, Bas Rabyah waited, ready to shove.

Jonah turned to Sartish one last time and raised a hand. "The Wind blow at your back."

Sartish almost returned the gesture, then dropped his hand

to his side. His dark eyes were fierce—too fierce. By contrast, the grief was naked in Jonah's eyes as he turned away. He nodded to Bas Rabyah. Together, they floated the boat. Bas joined Isabella at the oars, and Jonah took the helm. Once they passed the breakers, all the boats raised their sails, and the convoy drove east into the night.

* * *

When the moon rose, they lowered the sails and formed the boats into a circle. The People held up torches according to the custom—a ring of fire that played over the rippling black water. Curled up in the bow with her knees pulled up, Isabella wanted to bury her face, but forced herself to watch in silence as men from the other boats clambered on board and helped lower Disagree's body into the water.

At last, she rose to her feet with everyone else, unsteady with the movements of the hull.

"He survived the Ordeal of Windfire," Jonah said, looking around the circle, "and he gave his life for others. He is worthy!"

Voices echoed back, and Isabella raised her voice above theirs: "He is worthy!"

She was crying again, her tears gleaming in the torchlight. Close by her side, Shantih hugged her tighter. Disagree's body had begun to sink. As it did, there was movement beneath the water. A small group of mermaids surfaced, forming up around Disagree to escort him to the Sleepers. Jonah recognized the leader from her wrinkled features and curly white hair. "Queen Ruzhivo," he said. "We meet again."

The queen inclined her head. "Indeed we do, Elder Jonah. Properly, this time."

"Thank you for honoring his death," Jonah said, indicating Disagree.

"Of course," Queen Ruzhivo said. "He will rest with the others until it is time to wake."

"Wake?" Isabella whispered.

Queen Ruzhivo looked at her. "You do not think that this time is all there is, do you?"

Isabella shook her head, still crying. "No . . . At least, I couldn't . . ."

"This is just the beginning," Queen Ruzhivo said gently. "You will embrace him again."

Isabella nodded, wiping her eyes.

Queen Ruzhivo addressed Jonah. "The old man, Pierre. We took him also."

Isabella lowered her eyes. Ruzhivo noticed, and shook her head. "It was unexpected for you, but not for us. He did not force his fate. It was his time. However, he held something, and would not let it go."

Isabella looked up. "The Lamp!"

The mermaid inclined her head. "It was not given to us to touch, so we wrapped him with it. It is sleeping with him."

"That's as it should be," Jonah said.

Queen Ruzhivo nodded. "Until the Higher Mysterion."

"Until the Higher Mysterion," Jonah repeated.

The mermaid queen and her retinue sank out of sight, guiding the white-shrouded bulk of Disagree into the dark depths.

"What do we do now?" Isabella said.

Jonah turned to her. His eyes shone. "We make another Lamp."

Bas Rabyah started. "Another one! As the Elder did before?"

Jonah nodded.

"That will take many years," Bas Rabyah warned. "We had to go to the four corners of the world to assemble it . . ."

"Perhaps so," Jonah said. He was looking up at the dome of stars. "Or perhaps we may have some wings to help us."

"The Angeli?" Isabella said. "Do you think they will? They already stuck their necks out for us more than they should."

After returning them to the plateau, Azrel had decided to return above-the-heavens.

"I need to do some bowing and scraping," Azrel told them. "Try to make sure we're not completely cut off. Not that I mind, but Shantiel has her friends . . . Do you think you can manage on your own for a bit?"

Jonah smiled. "We'll try. And if we need you back, we'll just get ourselves into trouble."

Azrel rolled her eyes. "See you then, I suppose."

Jonah replied now: "I'm sure they'll come when we need them." He looked around the torch-lit circle, the faces of men and women young and old, of children huddling close to their parents. "The People of the Wind were one. But they were divided and scattered, and now they are more so than ever. We must bring them together again from their corners, from their hiding places. And once we're together again, we will use the new Lamp, and cast out those who would burn up the beauty of our world."

There were nods, and a few cheers, but they were disheartened, exhausted, a people wandering without a home. By contrast, Isabella felt a new strength welling up inside her. The dark grief of losing Disagree would always be there, but so would he—the rock who had always stood at her back. And if the mermaids and Jonah were right, she would throw her arms around him again, in the Higher Mysterion.

Whatever that is, she thought.

"What are we waiting for then?" she said, with a touch of impatience. "Let's go!"

"Soon," Jonah said. "First, we'll find a place to rest, and wait."

"Wait?" Isabella said. "What for?"

"I don't know," Jonah said. "But I do know that if you stay still long enough, everything will come to you in the end."

Isabella smiled. She grabbed his hand, lifted it to her lips, and kissed it. "Then I suppose we had better start waiting."

The End

Did you enjoy this book? You can make a big difference!

Reviews are the most powerful tools that I have when it comes to getting attention to my books. Although I'm not a starving artist, I don't have the financial muscle to take out full page ads in the *New York Times*.

But I do have something more powerful than that.

A committed, excited, and loyal group of readers.

Honest reviews of my book help bring it to the attention of new readers. The more reviews it has, the more Amazon "notices" it. At a certain point of interest, the Amazon algorithm can actually help make my books "more discoverable."

If you've enjoyed my novel, I invite you join my Reader Group by signing up here: http://eepurl.com/cTN5X1

I would also be very grateful if you'd spend only five minutes to leave a short review on the book's Amazon and Goodreads page. You can jump straight to that page by clicking below:

amazon.com/author/www.richardgarciamorgan.com

https://www.goodreads.com/rgarciamorgan

Thank you very much!